"WHAT DO MEN SEE WHEN THEY LOOK AT YOU, Georgia?"

It took her a moment to decide if she wanted to answer him, but she did. "They see the De Witt fortune."

Levi shook his head and took a step closer. "You're a very beautiful and desirable woman. I can't imagine there's a man alive who looks at you and thinks about money. Do you know what I see when I look at you?"

"What?"

"I see the afternoon sky in your eyes." His thumb stroked her cheek. "I hear the morning breeze in your voice." The pad of his thumb rubbed across her lower lip as a purr vibrated in the back of her throat. Desire rushed to his groin. "I feel the heat of your passion whenever we're close."

She swayed toward him. "You do?"

The slight redness of her lower lip, where she had bitten it, was too much for him. He had to taste Georgia, just once in his life. "I see all that, and much, much more." He lowered his head and claimed her mouth.

Desire ripped through his body as she raised her arms and twined them around his neck. He had only wanted to taste her sweetness, but as she pressed her breasts against his chest and deepened the kiss, he devoured her with his mouth. He couldn't get enough. He needed more. Wanted more . . .

WHAT ARE *LOVESWEPT* ROMANCES?

They are stories of true romance and touching emotion. We believe those two very important ingredients are constants in our highly sensual and very believable stories in the LOVE-SWEPT line. Our goal is to give you, the reader, stories of consistently high quality that may sometimes make you laugh, sometimes make you cry, but are always fresh and creative and contain many delightful surprises within their pages.

Most romance fans read an enormous number of books. Those they truly love, they keep. Others may be traded with friends and soon forgotten. We hope that each LOVESWEPT romance will be a treasure—a "keeper." We will always try to publish

LOVE STORIES YOU'LL NEVER FORGET
BY AUTHORS YOU'LL ALWAYS REMEMBER

The Editors

Loveswept ® 842

White Lace & Promises:

GEORGIA ON HIS MIND

MARCIA EVANICK

BANTAM BOOKS
NEW YORK · TORONTO · LONDON · SYDNEY · AUCKLAND

WHITE LACE & PROMISES: GEORGIA ON HIS MIND
A Bantam Book / July 1997

ISBN 0-553-44586-3

Published simultaneously in the United States and Canada

PRINTED IN THE UNITED STATES OF AMERICA

OPM   10 9 8 7 6 5 4 3 2 1

PROLOGUE

Georgia De Witt frowned at the reflection staring back at her from the floor-to-ceiling mirror. She looked beautiful. The white satin and lace wedding gown that fit her body with such perfection was breathtakingly exquisite. For the price the White Lace and Promises Bridal Boutique was charging her older brother, Morgan, who insisted on paying for her wedding, a small Third World country should have come with it. So why didn't it feel right? Maybe it wasn't the gown. Maybe it was her impending marriage. Did she really want to marry a man who felt more like another brother than a lover?

A couple of startled gasps and the sudden quiet of the fitting room penetrated her troubled thoughts. She glanced in the mirror and was shocked to see that her fiancé, Adam Young, had entered the large room crowded with seam-stresses and her entire bridal party.

"Excuse me, everyone, but I need a few moments alone with Georgia," Adam said.

"Sir, I must demand that you leave immediately!" exclaimed the owner, Cleo Bodine.

"It's all right, Cleo. He's my fiancé." Georgia slowly turned away from the mirror to study the sole man in the fitting room. She had never seen Adam look so upset or purposeful. "Could we have a moment of privacy?" she asked the room full of women. "Please." Anxious whispers and scurrying feet answered her request.

"He's not supposed to see you in the gown before the wedding," cried Vanessa, one of her bridesmaids and the only person who hadn't fled the room. "It's bad luck."

Georgia watched wistfully as Vanessa raised the hem of her yellow gown and fled the room after receiving a glare from Adam. She would have loved to follow her friend. Her gut instincts were telling her she wasn't going to like whatever Adam had come to say.

"You look beautiful in that gown."

She raised one light blond, perfectly shaped eyebrow at the absurdity of his statement. "That's not what you barged in here to tell me, Adam."

"No, it's not."

His long silence caused the hair on the back of her neck to stand up. She stiffened as he moved a few steps closer, and finally said, "Georgia, I can't marry you."

Damn! What am I going to tell the caterers? Georgia's eyes widened in shock, not only at Adam's declaration, but also at her ridiculous thoughts about caterers. *Shouldn't my heart be breaking? And why in the hell do I feel like sighing in relief instead of crying?* She blinked rapidly. Maybe this was all some silly misunderstanding. "Why not?"

He took a deep breath. "I don't love you."

"How do you know?" She had been wondering if she really loved Adam, or if the thought of getting married was what she had been looking forward to these past months. Adam's kisses were nice, but they didn't heat her blood or stir her soul. Had he felt that lack of desire too?

He gave her a small crooked smile. "I would know."

"You've met someone else, haven't you?" For the past week he had been acting awfully peculiarly.

"Yes."

"Last week, right?" Damn, now she was beginning to get angry. It was one thing to call off the wedding because he didn't love her. It was totally different to call it off because he'd found someone else. What did this other woman have that she didn't?

"You knew?" he asked, obviously surprised.

"You've been awfully busy this past week, and

you barely kissed my cheek good night when you did manage a couple of hours for me." Her eyes narrowed at the thought of Adam making love to another woman, especially since she and Adam had never gotten past first base. "What's her name?"

"Emily."

"Emily what?" She couldn't think of a single Emily she and Adam knew, besides Emily Harrison who was eighty-two, if a day, and who lived alone with her butler in a huge mansion filled with antiques, dolls, and cats.

"I don't know," Adam answered. He shrugged. "I seem to have lost her."

The despair in his voice caused her to blink. "Pardon?"

"I only met her once and she didn't tell me her last name."

"Did she tell you anything at all?" She was being dumped for a woman he'd met once and then lost? Lord, could this day possibly get any worse?

"I know she lives in the county, is a widow, and that she has three . . . " The last word was an unintelligible croak.

"Three what?" Georgia asked. "Cats? Alligators? Eyes?" Oh Lord, for one wild moment she thought he had said children. Adam loathed children. It was one of the few subjects about their future they had discussed. Adam didn't want any children, which was fine by her. She'd never felt a deep desire to have one.

"*Children.* She has three children."

Tears of mirth filled her eyes, and she released a very unladylike bark of laughter just as the curtains were yanked aside and her brother, Morgan, barged into the fitting room.

"What in the hell is going on here?" Morgan demanded. "Vanessa just told me you're calling off the wedding, Young!"

Georgia scowled at the thought of her bridesmaids eavesdropping on their conversation, then she stepped between Adam and her brother. Morgan looked ready to rip Adam to shreds. Adam was being punished enough for the grief he was causing her. She couldn't imagine him falling in love with a woman who had three children. There seemed to be a sweet justice, after all. "Now, Morgan," she began.

Morgan gently, but purposely, pushed her aside. "Did you or did you not call off the wedding, Young?"

She cringed at the volume of her brother's question. Morgan never raised his voice. He usually got what he wanted without resorting to that level of emotion. She had seen grown men shudder and quake at just his stare.

She saw Adam square his shoulders, then he calmly said, "I called off the wedding, Morgan."

Her brother's fist shot out so fast, it was a blur. She watched horrified as Adam went flying backward to land on his butt in a sea of white silk and lace. She had taken a concerned step toward him when Morgan grabbed her wrist and dragged her from the room. Her last glimpse of her now ex-fiancé was of him grimacing as he touched his already red eye.

ONE

Levi Horst slowly turned his pickup truck onto the gravel driveway, and followed the drive around the side of the house to the garage in back. He parked beside a yellow rental truck and frowned. Georgia De Witt, the person currently paying for his carpentry skills, was back early. He hadn't been expecting her until sometime in the late afternoon. Then again, he hadn't been expecting a lot of things that had happened recently.

The last thing he had been expecting was to become a father. But that was what he was now. He was legally and morally the guardian to his sixteen-year-old nephew, Shane Edward Weaver, who on his arrival at the Harrisburg airport the previous afternoon had informed Levi he only answered to one name, Seaweed.

Levi had spent the rest of the afternoon and

evening trying to have a conversation with Shane and trying not to be rude by staring at the rebellious teen and his bizarre attire. He probably would have developed less of a headache whacking his head against a cement wall. He couldn't bring himself to call his sister's only child Seaweed, and Shane refused to answer to anything else.

To Levi's mind, the mule his grandfather had owned when Levi was a boy had been less stubborn. One day Jack the Ass, as his grandfather had called the mule, stopped in the middle of plowing and refused to move for three whole days. Neighbors from miles around came by to see the sight and good-naturedly poke fun at Grandfather. Two weeks later the mule had been sold to a farmer in a neighboring county who hadn't heard the story, and Grandfather went out and bought himself a sweet-natured plow horse named Lilly.

In Levi's opinion both Lilly and Jack the Ass had been a far better sight than his nephew. What in the world had happened to the happy and loving boy he had known for years? The last time he saw Shane he was withdrawn and silent, but that was to be expected, considering the circumstances. The black-suited fifteen-year-old boy had been attending his parents' funeral. In the past seven months Shane had had a birthday and was now on his third guardian. Levi's sister, Caroline, must be rattling heaven's gate to get back to her little boy.

Caroline and her husband, Ben, had moved to Littleport, Iowa, where Ben's family lived, immediately after their wedding. Levi had visited them a few times over the years, and they had annually come back to Lancaster County, Pennsylvania, to visit her family. He had loved and missed his sister, but he knew where her heart lay, with her husband and son. Then, seven months ago Caroline and Ben lost their lives in a tragic barn fire while they tried to save their trapped livestock. Thankfully, Shane had been in school or he might have also perished with his parents.

Ben's older brother and his wife had opened their arms and home to Shane. Levi had thought it was a good idea, considering they already had three children of their own and it meant Shane wouldn't have to change schools or move away from his hometown. They had promised Levi he would always be welcomed there as Shane's uncle. Two months later he received word that Shane was being moved to his grandparents' home, on Ben's side of the family. Levi never learned exactly what had happened, only that this arrangement would be better for Shane. Since he was in Pennsylvania and Caroline had never had anything but praise for her husband's family, he didn't question the decision.

Yesterday afternoon was the first time he had seen Shane since the funeral, and he hadn't recognized the boy. Shane's own mother wouldn't have recognized him. The whole silent drive home from the airport he had called himself seven different kinds of fool for not visiting the boy and seeing for himself how he was faring. How had the happy, outgoing, straight-A student changed into the sulky, dog-collar-wearing, pierced-eared adolescent? He had shaved off most of his brown hair, leaving only a spiked Mohawk that had to be a good five inches high and glistened with enough gel to lubricate every squeaky wheel in the county. He wore a silver skull earring in his left ear and in his right he boasted six different earrings. They ranged from silver hoops and a gold dolphin to a four-inch dangling bare-breasted mermaid that bordered on being obscene.

Three days earlier when Shane's grandparents had called and practically begged him to take the boy, Levi had been shocked. Shane was Ben's boy and they had thought the world revolved around Ben. When Levi pressured them about why they were willing to release custody of their grandson, all they said was Shane was going through a difficult time and perhaps needed a stronger male influence in his life than his seventy-one-year-old grandfather. Levi had agreed immediately, then had anxiously awaited "fatherhood" and Shane's arrival. He had been totally unprepared for "Seaweed."

Levi stared at Georgia's old garage and wearily rubbed his face with his hands. Sleep had been a long time coming last night. At five o'clock that morning he had been awakened by a noise outside. When he went to investigate, he found Shane sitting alone in the dark on the wooden deck that faced the woods. His heart had gone out to the boy, and for one fleeting moment he'd felt his nephew's pain. When he tried to comfort the boy, he was shoved aside and told in no uncertain terms to "get bent." While he stood there trying to decide if he should wash Shane's mouth out with soap or ground him, the boy disappeared back inside the house, slamming and locking his bedroom door. Loud screeching, clashing, banging sounds masquerading as music vibrated the walls until it was time to take his nephew to Cocalico High School to be registered for the upcoming school year and to receive his introductory tour.

The tour had not gone smoothly, and when Levi dropped Shane back at the house they had had a heated argument over what was appropriate conduct. For the first time since he'd started his carpentry business eight years earlier, Levi not only was late to the job site, but also really didn't want to be there. He'd much rather be at home talking to Shane and coming to some type of understanding about how they were going to live with each other for the next couple of years. After the way they had just parted company, though, Levi figured it would be more prudent to give both himself and Shane a cooling-off period. That night would be soon enough to start hammering out any agreements. That is if Shane would talk to him without being referred to as Seaweed.

Levi got out of the truck, reached for his tool belt lying on the seat next to him, and headed for the house. He had a kitchen to remodel before he could start on the main project, converting Georgia De Witt's barn into an antique shop. Sitting in his truck and brooding about a certain baggy jean–wearing teenager who thought it was cool to show the world the top of his boxer shorts wasn't going to get the job done.

What he needed to do was to concentrate on work. He had another mouth to feed, and if Shane's current wardrobe was any indication, a very expensive shopping trip for some back-to-school clothes and supplies.

He walked around to the front door and knocked. He had Georgia's spare key to the house, but he didn't want to waltz in unannounced. The past several days, while she had been away on business, he had used the key without hesitation and had accomplished a lot of work. Now that she was back he would knock first and spend twice as long completing whatever he was doing. It never failed. As soon as she walked into a room his hands turned into ten thumbs and his mind conjured up erotic images. None of which had to do with work, and all centering on his employer.

Never again would he accept a job working for a beautiful single woman in her home. It was too damn distracting. Georgia De Witt wasn't just beautiful, she was a gorgeous fantasy woman. The woman had everything; a face that could definitely launch a thousand ships and a body with more curves than a circle. Her voice was light and sweet and could slip down a man's spine and make him go hard just thinking about what it would sound like thickened with passion. Georgia carried charm, grace, and class the way most women carried their pocketbooks. She was well educated, highly intelligent, and possessed a business savvy that any Fortune 500 company would pay handsomely for. She was also one of the sweetest, nicest, most down-to-earth people he had ever met. And that bothered him more than he liked to admit.

Georgia had absolutely no right being so nice. She should have been some stuck-up society girl who wouldn't give him, the hired hand, the time of day. Instead she brought him glasses of iced tea on hot summer days and invited him to lunch more times than he cared to count, until she finally realized he wasn't going to accept the invitations and stopped asking. Once, on her way home from somewhere she had stopped to buy herself an ice-cream cone and bought him one, too, so she wouldn't feel rude eating in front of him. He'd had to accept the double-dip chocolate cone or feel like something he'd scrape off the bottom of his shoe.

At first he'd thought she was playing some

sick game with him; rich society girl with time on her hands dallies with lowly carpenter. But during the past several weeks he'd come to realize she was that nice to everyone, and he'd had a good laugh at himself for his overinflated ego—or was it wishful thinking? He refused to spend a lot of time examining his feelings on the subject.

He listened to the silence from inside the house and jiggled his key ring. Maybe Georgia wasn't home. There was a very good chance she was already out somewhere, perhaps at one of the other two antique shops she owned in the southern part of the county. He raised his hand once again, just to make sure, and this time knocked louder.

Georgia's voice reached him through the open windows. "Come in, Levi! What are you waiting for, the butler to open the door for you?"

He frowned as he turned the knob and stepped into the living room. It sounded as if his sweet-tempered employer had gotten up on the wrong side of the bed. He took three steps into the room, then halted at the sight that greeted him. Georgia's perfectly shaped tush was bouncing slightly in the air as she leaned into a cardboard box. He swallowed hard and wished he'd never connected Georgia and a bed in the same thought. Temptation was wearing khaki-colored shorts and a pair of long tanned legs built to wrap around a man's waist. He was in trouble. Deep trouble.

"Do you know which box has the coffee in it?" she asked without raising her head out of the box she was searching.

Levi glanced around the room and almost laughed. Three days earlier, when Georgia had left for some estate sales in West Virginia, he had moved everything out of her kitchen into her living room, including all the boxes she had packed. The room had been crowded, but orderly. Now it looked as if a gang of thieves had trashed the place. His neatly stacked boxes were scattered around the room, standing open on the couch, the chairs, and even the kitchen table. Boxes of crackers and noodles were on the coffee table. Glasses and plates were piled on top of the television. A soup ladle and egg timer sat on one of the wooden kitchen chairs. Potholders and tea towels were everywhere.

"I never realized," he said as he walked over to the last two boxes that weren't torn open, "that you were one of those people who needed caffeine to start your day."

"That's because by the time you arrive I usually have half a pot in me." Georgia straightened up and arched her back.

He quickly turned away from the enticing view and folded back the flaps on the first box. "All that caffeine isn't good for you." He pulled out the blue can of ground coffee and held it out to her.

She snatched the can from him. "Neither is

smoking, but millions of people still do it." She grinned at the coffeemaker, sitting on top of the microwave. With a flick of her wrist she pulled out the brown filter basket and groaned. "Oh, no. I need the filters now!" She frantically looked around and groaned louder. "I'm never going to find them in this mess."

She wore such a look of dejection, he had to suppress a smile. He bent down and pulled the filters from the same box the coffee had been in. "I take it you had your daily pot of coffee in you when you packed up your kitchen."

She grabbed the filters, slapped one into the basket, and proceeded to dump in the coffee grounds without even measuring. "I could have used you about half an hour ago." She dumped a pot full of water into the machine and gleefully flipped the switch.

"Sorry about being late." He thrust a hand through his hair and wondered what else he was supposed to say. "You won't be charged for the time."

She glanced up from the box she had been searching through. A coffee cup was clenched in each fist. "I wasn't worried about being charged for the time, Levi. You could have saved me a half hour of searching for the coffee and another hour or so to restore this room." She swung one of the cobalt blue mugs in the general direction of the chaos surrounding them. "How is it that you know where everything is and I don't?"

"Could be because I moved it all in here and I did put it in a generally neat order." He pointed to the boxes beside him. "These boxes are all your food stuff." He moved his finger to point to the other side of the refrigerator. "Those are your dishes." His finger moved once again. "And that's your pots, pans, and such."

Georgia looked around her in amazement. "Are you always so organized?"

"It saves time, especially when you're looking for something."

"Like coffee?"

He matched her smile with one of his own. "Like coffee."

She seemed momentarily surprised. "You should do that more often." She reached for the now-filled pot and poured two cups of coffee.

"What? Point out your cookie sheets and frying pans?"

She handed him one of the mugs. "No, I was referring to your smile. You have a beautiful smile." She reached inside the refrigerator and held out the milk to him.

There was something so damn intimate about her knowing how he took his coffee. Intimate and scary. If he didn't count the occasional waitress, the last woman who'd poured his morning coffee had been his wife. His ex-wife. He took the milk and splashed some into his coffee before handing it back to Georgia. "Thanks." He didn't bother clarifying if he was thanking her for the milk or for the comment about his smile. Hell, he didn't have anything to smile about, and he better start remembering that. Georgia was his employer and nowhere in that relationship was there room for him to be sharing a cozy cup of coffee in her crowded living room. His butt belonged in the hollow shell of what once was her kitchen.

"The flooring company called yesterday," he said. "They'll be installing the kitchen floor next Thursday." He walked through the opening into the completely gutted twelve-by-twenty-two-foot room. Bare two-by-fours, particle board flooring, and an open rafter ceiling greeted him.

Georgia followed him into the room and glanced around. "Are you going to be ready for them?"

"The only thing I need is your choice of color for the paint." He finished the coffee, set the empty mug on the windowsill, and started to work exactly where he had left off the day before. Electrical wiring wasn't bad. It was plumbing that he disliked. "The plumbers I subcontracted will be here tomorrow morning at seven."

"I'll stop by the hardware store this afternoon and look over the paint chips." She walked over to the newly installed windows and glanced out at the corn field beyond. She then walked over to the dining area of the room and studied the view from the pair of double-hungs and the patio doors he had installed. "The bigger windows and patio doors really lighten up the room, don't they?"

He glanced up from the electrical wire he was unwinding from its box. "Windows generally do that." Lord, he wished she would leave so he could get some work done. There was something about her beautiful blond hair when she pulled it into a ponytail. It exposed the back of her delicate neck and gave his undisciplined gaze just one more place to land on. The woman was driving him straight out of his hormone-propelled mind, and she hadn't a clue about what she was doing. She was standing there talking about windows and sunlight and he was semiaroused just because she was in the same room.

"I hauled your washer and dryer out onto the back porch," he said as he bent his head and continued to unroll the wire. "I'm afraid you're not going to be able to do any laundry here for about a week. I should have the laundry room finished by then."

"That will be fine." She turned away from the doors. "I have to go to my two shops today to deliver the stuff I picked up on my trip." She hesitated by the doorway. "If you need me, I'll be stopping at the Lancaster shop first, then the one in Strasburg."

He grunted something that he hoped sounded like, "No problem," as he pulled another ten feet of wire from the box.

"Bye."

He gave another noncommittal grunt without looking up. A minute later he heard the front door shut. He dropped the wire and wiped his sweaty hands down the sides of his jeans. *If you need me!* Common sense told him she had been talking about the renovations. His body was telling him something completely different.

His body was telling him it had been one hell of a long time since he'd been with a woman and hell, yes he needed her. Why, after all these years, had his body finally reawakened to the fact that he was still a man in the most basic sense of the word? And why had it been Georgia De Witt who'd stirred it back to life?

He closed his eyes and willed his body to obey his command to ignore Georgia's existence. Taking a deep breath, he counted to twenty before he heard the big rental truck start up.

Quickly, he moved away from the patio door and leaned against one of the two-by-fours to watch as Georgia backed the yellow truck down the drive. She looked so young and tiny sitting behind the wheel of that big truck. He'd be amazed if no police officer pulled her over just to make sure she had a driver's license.

He looked down at the hundred feet of wire he had yanked from the box and groaned. He only needed enough wire for a ten-foot run. What in the hell was he going to do about Georgia? The way he was going he would be totally out of his mind by the time he hooked up her stove. He was never going to make it through the entire job, finishing her house and then renovating the barn into a antique shop, with his sanity intact.

TWO

Georgia parked her Ford Explorer next to Levi's pickup truck and glanced around at her home. Her home. She liked the sound of that. She loved her home . . . almost. Total admiration and love would come as soon as Levi had finished his long and impressive list of things to do. The renovations were going to cost her more than the amount she had paid for the house, barn, and surrounding six acres of corn fields. The farmer up the road had paid a small fee to the elderly couple who had owned the property before her to farm the fields. She liked the idea of her antiques shop being surrounded by corn fields, so she had kept the same arrangement.

She looked at the barn and smiled. It was an old bank barn constructed from fieldstone and thick oak beams. The wood exterior was a washed-out red with flaking white trim. Four faded hex signs, once used to protect against evil spirits, were barely visible. Levi had promised to bring the once brilliantly colored designs back to their original glory. It was one of the reasons she had hired him to do the work. When she had given him a tour of the barn and house, he had understood exactly what she was looking for. He had understood the need to preserve as much of the past as possible.

She had interviewed four different contractors before she contacted Levi. At first she had been hesitant to call him because he worked alone and that meant the job would take longer to complete, but his references were outstanding. He was known for preserving the atmosphere of the past, while incorporating modern conveniences. As they'd walked around her barn, she had tried to convey her expectations and ideas. He had not only understood exactly what she was saying, but also tossed out a couple of ideas that had astounded her. By the time the tour of the house had been completed, she was ready to hire him. Levi Horst was capable of fulfilling her dream.

At least, he was capable of fulfilling her dream for her house and newest shop. As for her other dreams . . .

Her smile faded as she glanced down at the passenger seat. A dozen strips of paint chips were scattered across the leather seat. After unloading at her two shops the "finds" she had bought in West Virginia, she had returned the rental truck, picked up her Explorer, and headed back home. Her one stop had been at the hardware store, where Levi had been picking up a lot of his materials. It had taken her exactly five minutes to decide which color to paint the kitchen, laundry room, and powder room. Curiosity, to see if Levi would pick the same shade of creamy butter, named Butterwick, had her taking the extra eleven strips home with her.

It was uncanny the way Levi's taste perfectly matched hers. So far the only item they had differed on was the brass faucet she had picked out for the sink in the master bathroom. Every morning as she brushed her teeth she couldn't help thinking that maybe Levi had been right. The brass and white porcelain faucet that he had pointed out twice might have looked better.

How could two people from totally different walks of life have the same taste?

Well, maybe referring to it as having the same taste was off the mark. They obviously had the same taste in cabinets and flooring. They even had the same vision of how to turn the barn into one of the county's top-rated antique shops. But there the similarities ended. For the past several weeks, as she had watched Levi rip down walls and reconstruct her bathroom with his bare hands, she had been dreaming about what else the man could do with those strong, work-roughened hands. Levi, however, never so much as gave her the time of day, unless she specifically asked for it.

He acted as if he would prefer she pack her bags and move elsewhere until the job was done.

Until this morning. This morning he had smiled.

The shock of seeing that magnificent smile on his strong-jawed face was still with her, hours later. So was the heat. Levi was a good-looking man whose attractiveness came from character, not from classic movie star looks. When that smile had curved his usually compressed lips, she had felt her stomach drop to her knees and her toes curl within her sneakers. Hollywood would make a bundle having that smile spread across a thirty-foot screen. Women would pay a fortune just to see how it lit up his deep brown eyes. And that morning, for one fleeting moment, it had been directed straight at her.

It had been totally hers.

Until he realized what he had done. Then the smile had fled and he'd gone to work as if she weren't there. It was the story of her life. Georgia the untouchable. Georgia with the dollar sign hung around her neck. Georgia the invisible.

She pulled herself away from any self-evaluations and, scooping up the paint-chip strips, headed for the house. If Levi didn't want to touch her, that was fine by her. She wasn't into throwing herself at men, but she'd be damned if she would act invisible around them.

Five minutes later she was standing in her crowded and totally disorganized living room staring at the kitchen table. Spread out across the wooden surface were the paint-chip cards, as well as the brochures for the cabinets and appliances she had ordered, and samples of the countertop and linoleum flooring she had picked. Now that she had everything in front of her, she might want to go with the paint color directly next to the one she had chosen under the glaring florescent light of the hardware store. French Creme had a touch less yellow than Butterwick.

"You're back."

She had heard Levi's heavy boots heading in her direction and wasn't startled by his voice, just the deepness of it. Lord, the man had a voice that had to start at his toes and work its way up his long legs and then rumble through that incredible chest. "I just walked in." She didn't bother to turn around and greet him. Between his voice, the disturbing dreams about his hands, and his killer smile from that morning, she was teetering on the edge of throwing herself at him.

"Did you pick a color yet?" he asked as he came to stand beside her.

"Yes." She was definitely going to go with the French Creme.

"Which one?" He glanced between the paint samples and the assorted brochures and samples.

"You tell me first which one you would pick." She quickly multiplied in her head. Twelve strips times five colors on each card. That was sixty different colors. What were the chances he would pick French Creme?

He studied each strip. "If I had to choose . . ." His hand hovered over the strip with Butterwick and French Creme on it. "I'd pick"—his finger was directly above Butterwick—"this one."

Her heart gave a funny little lurch as his finger landed on French Creme. She managed a smile. "Why that one?" Lord, this wasn't just coincidences any longer. This was downright frightening. The man had picked the exact color she had chosen. One chance out of sixty and he nailed it. She wondered if he ever played the lottery.

"I would have said Butterwick," he answered, "but I think with the flooring, cabinets, and countertops you picked, you might want something with a bit less yellow in it."

"Really?"

He frowned at the color sampler in his hand. "Well, that's just my asked-for opinion." He carefully placed the card on the table next to the other strips. "What color do you want me to paint the rooms?"

"French Creme."

"No, really. What color did you pick?" He lightly brushed the chip strips, spreading them out more evenly. "There're a number of colors here that would look good."

"I'm not interested in making the room look *good*. I want it to look great, along with warm, inviting, and homey. I had picked Butterwick in the store, but when you take it out from under the glare of fluorescent lights and place it next to everything already on order, it has just a touch too much yellow in it. French Creme was my choice too." For two cents she would have stuck with Butterwick, just to disagree with him, but she couldn't stand the fact that she would be walking into the room every morning for years to come and hating the too yellow walls. What did it really matter that he had the excellent taste to choose French Creme?

"Really?" Levi sounded as if he didn't know whether he should believe her.

"What color did you think I would pick?" She tapped a pale blue. "Swan Lake or"—her finger moved to a golden mist color—"Passion Sunrise?" She frowned down at the cards. "Who names these colors anyway?" Passion Sunrise? She had always associated passion with nighttime, not sunrise. Wasn't it the night that brought out lustful urges, not the dawn? When, or if, she ever spent a passion-filled night, she wanted to be too tired in the morning to notice if the sun even rose, let alone what color the sunrise was.

"It's probably some tie-wearing executive stuck in a corner office with a dictionary and a pile of paint chips."

" 'Silky Skies.' 'Two to Tango.' Sounds to me as if the guy has spent too much time alone in his office." She couldn't decide if the names sounded romantic or desperate. She shook her head and walked to the other end of the room to retrieve any messages from the answering machine. "Everything went okay today?"

Levi glanced up from the paint chips. He seemed to have been glaring at the last strip of colors. "Yes. I have to leave at five tonight."

Georgia felt her heart skip a beat. Her finger rested on the "play" button on her answering machine. Levi never left at five. Then again, he had never been late before either. Now that she thought about it, there was a new tension surrounding him. It appeared he had something laying heavy on his mind. That could mean only one thing. "Hot date?" she asked. Perhaps Levi wasn't as fancy-free as she had thought.

His frown turned into a scowl. "Personal."

Definitely a date. "It's okay, Levi. You don't have to clock in and out. I'm paying for the completion of the job, not by the hour. If you're leaving at five, that's fine." So he didn't want her to know he had a date. Nothing wrong with that. The man obviously wasn't the kind to kiss and tell. The last thing she needed was Levi confiding his love life to her. It was depressing enough just to know he had one.

He hesitated for a moment before saying, "I'll go finish cleaning up."

"Fine, see you in the morning." She kept her back toward him and pressed the "play" button. The first message was from her brother, Morgan.

He apologized for not being in the office when she had called earlier to see if she could take him to lunch. The second message was from Clint Halloway apologizing once again for his behavior the other Saturday night when he had too much to drink and had been feeling a little "frisky." He wanted to take her to dinner and was eagerly awaiting her return call. Clint Halloway would be waiting until hell froze over.

The last message was from Francine, the manager of her shop in Lancaster. She had taken Georgia's advice and called Mrs. Peterman about the pine cupboard Georgia had picked up at one of the estate sales in West Virginia. Mrs. Peterman had not only bought the cupboard sight unseen, but also planned to stop by the shop tomorrow morning to see what else had come in. The message brought a smile to Georgia's face.

No one could dispute she was her brother's sister. The De Witts had a reputation for being shrewd in business. Morgan's life revolved around the asphalt business their parents had left them sixteen years earlier, when they were both killed in an automobile accident. Over the years Morgan had taken the small family business and turned it into a huge corporation. Her brother wouldn't rest, it seemed, until every road in America was paved with De Witt's Asphalt. She, on the other hand, liked to spend her time preserving and appreciating the past.

Asphalt and antiques were on opposite ends of

the spectrum, but as she liked to tease her brother, at least they had the first letter in common.

"I'm leaving now," Levi said as he reentered the living room. "Remember, the plumbers will be here by seven in the morning and I'll probably be arriving a half hour before that."

"I'll be up." She was half tempted to tell Levi to use his key and wake her when he had the coffee ready. She knew it went beyond simple politeness to make sure the carpenter working on her house had his morning coffee. But she couldn't bring herself to rudely drink her morning quota of caffeine in front of him.

She watched as he walked out the front door and softly closed it behind him. The man hadn't looked as if he were headed for a hot date or a wild night out on the town, she mused. He had looked tense enough to snap in half if he got slammed by a strong wind. She found herself wondering what was on his mind. Whatever it was, it didn't appear to agree with him.

She glanced around the living room and knew what was going to kill a good portion of her evening. The room was a disaster from her frantic search for coffee. It was going to take at least an hour to reorganize the room, then she had to scrounge up something for dinner. It was a good thing she'd had a large lunch. Dinner looked as if it was going to be a light affair.

The color brochures and paint samples caught

her eye and drew her back to them. She was curious about why Levi had been frowning at the last strip of colors. The cardboard strip was assorted shades of pale peach that she had barely glanced at in the hardware store. She knew instinctively which color had been his focus, but she couldn't determine why it had caused such a reaction. Nestled in between Scarboro Peach and Peachtree Plaza was a shade of peach called Dawn over Georgia.

Levi turned off Texter Mountain Road and onto the gravel lane that led to his home. Home! He liked the sound of that. Ten years earlier he had built the three-bedroom log house three-quarters of the way up the side of the mountain; as far away from civilization as humanly possible, yet still in the county that he loved. Lancaster County, with its broad valleys and gently flowing streams, had captured the hearts of its earlier settlers, the Pennsylvania Dutch, as easily as it had captured his. He couldn't imagine anywhere else he would rather live.

Ten years ago he'd needed the peace that Texter Mountain offered. He'd needed the quiet and the tranquility of the surrounding woods. He'd needed to heal and to forget. He wasn't sure if he had accomplished either. He wasn't sure if he ever would.

He slowed the truck to a halt as a pair of

squirrels darted across the lane. Ten years ago he had been a father, and no blood test would ever tell him differently. Jennifer, with her mop of red curls and sweet smile, had called him 'Da-da." She had loved to be tickled and thought the funniest thing on earth was watching her six-feet, one-inch tall father crawl around behind the furniture and play peekaboo with her. In his eyes Jenny would always be twelve months and four days old. The exact age she'd been the last time he saw her, the day his ex-wife drove away with her lover, with Jenny strapped in the car seat, crying her eyes out and calling for her da-da. The day his heart had been ripped from his chest.

He never should have married his high school sweetheart. Everyone had said so. His parents, his sister, even his best man had tried to talk him out of it. He had loved Christine, with all her faults, but had never told anyone the real reason behind the rushed wedding. Christine was pregnant, or so she had told him. It turned out she wasn't, but by then it was too late. They were already man and wife. He had been willing to make the best of it—after all, he loved her—and over the next several years the marriage shaked, rattled, and rolled along. Christine didn't like to be tied down, and their on-again, off-again marriage all but destroyed what love he had felt for her. The next thing he knew Christine was pregnant, and he was going to be a father. His love for Christine never rekindled, but he was willing to stay married for

Jenny's sake. He loved his daughter from the moment the nurse placed her in his arms.

Christine's flirting ways grew along with her unhappiness. One day, before Jenny's first birthday, Christine announced she was leaving with her lover. Levi told her to go, but he was keeping Jenny. That was the day he learned he wasn't Jenny's biological father. He fought it, not believing her, until the blood test proved Christine right. He fought it until Christine took the sobbing girl from his arms and strapped her into the car seat and drove off. Then he just didn't have the strength to fight any longer. Jenny was gone, and she had taken his heart with her.

He glanced up the lane, but knew he wouldn't be able to see his house. There were too many bends and twists in the drive. The other night when Ben's parents had called and asked him to take his nephew, he had felt a stirring in the empty hole inside his chest. Blood and muscle had joined with hope. He was going to be a father again.

He knew he could never take the place of Shane's real father, but it was something. Someone needed him, or so he had thought. Shane didn't need him, though. If Shane's words and actions could be believed, not only was he not needed, he wasn't wanted.

His life was like the twisted lane he had bulldozed ten years ago. He had gone from being a surrogate father of a sweet smiling one-year-old girl who called him "Da-da," to being the legal guardian of a rebellious sixteen-year-old boy who so far had called him "yo" and "Unc."

Fatherhood had been yanked away from him before. This time he was holding the custody papers, and he wasn't about to give up on Shane. It was time to open his heart and home to something besides his bitterness and pain. Shane had a lot more healing to do than Levi himself ever had. Shane had lost both his parents to the fire and apparently now his uncle, aunt, three cousins, and a set of grandparents to his defiant attitude.

Levi started back up the drive. Tonight he'd take Shane out for pizza, and then maybe they would hit the mall. All teenagers liked pizza and shopping, didn't they?

He turned the last bend in the road and sighed as loud music shattered the quiet surrounding his home. Shane was sitting on the front porch that overlooked the valley below. It was a breathtaking view that made all the extra trouble he had gone through to build the house on this particular spot well worth it. A person could see for miles, and this late summer evening was particularly beautiful. He parked the truck and headed for the porch. Obviously Shane didn't agree with him about the view. The boy's eyes were closed, as if he were sleeping, but that had to be impossible with the noise coming from the large black box sitting next to his feet.

Levi clamped his teeth together, climbed the

two steps up to the porch, and sat in the rocker next to his nephew. "Shane, do you mind lowering that some?"

Shane didn't even flinch. His eyes remained closed, but Levi knew he wasn't sleeping.

"Shane!" His voice rose above the blaring music. No response. His voice and his temper rose even higher. "Shane!" When the boy still pretended he wasn't there, Levi reached over and pressed the "power" button. Instant silence.

Shane opened his eyes and glared at his uncle.

Levi felt the boy's hatred curl into his stomach. Tonight, after Shane was in bed, he was calling the boy's uncle and grandparents in Iowa to see what in the hell had been going on back there. This was not the same boy he had known since birth. This was not his sister's loving son who swiped chocolate chip cookies faster than she could bake them. "Sorry, but I asked nice the first time for you to turn it down."

"I like it loud." Shane reached down and pressed the "power" button. He once more closed his eyes and ignored his uncle as blaring music rattled the porch.

Levi's temper was dangerously ready to explode. He turned off the CD player again, then yanked the electrical cord from the outlet under the window.

Shane cracked open his eyes a slit and looked at the black cord snaked across the wooden floorboard. He didn't say a word.

"If you have to have the music so loud that it not only rattles the glass in the windows but scares every animal off the mountain, I think it's time to have your ears checked." Levi managed a smile as Shane raised his hateful gaze to him. "The school gave us a stack of paperwork this morning. During my lunch break I glanced through most of it and noticed there's a physical form in there. The state requires all eleventh graders to have a physical. Should I make an appointment with my doctor, or do you have a certain preference?"

He honestly didn't think there was anything wrong with Shane's hearing. Teenagers were notorious for listening to loud music. He'd listened to loud music himself when he was a teenager. But he couldn't remember its being that loud, or that awful sounding. The physical was a good excuse to begin a conversation about the upcoming school year. Shane had to be anxious and uneasy about starting eleventh grade in a different school and without knowing a soul. Shane needed to make some friends.

The boy stood up, picked up his CD player, and tromped into the house without saying a word. The slamming of the screen door said it all.

Levi ignored the loud bang and concentrated on the magnificent view. It had always soothed him in the past, it would do it again. All he needed was to count to ten, and the frustration rippling through his body would disappear.

It took counting to 120 before his breath came slow, easy, and measured, but it worked. He wasn't going to let Shane get to him. No matter how many buttons the boy managed to push.

Levi forced himself to think of something besides Shane. Work. Work was always a good subject. He loved his work and never accepted a job that he disliked. His current job was no exception. When it was finished, Georgia De Witt's house was going to be superb. The woman had excellent taste, and obviously the money to match. Everything she'd ordered was top-notch, and no expense had been spared.

He couldn't wait until the kitchen was done so he could start on the barn. When she had shown him the barn and started to explain how she saw its being converted into an antique shop, he had understood perfectly what she had in mind. He had stood in the middle of the hay-strewn, cobweb-encrusted barn and seen the exclusive shop. He'd envisioned the haylofts being transformed into additional showrooms and had even offered a few suggestions of his own. Georgia had been with him all the way. He hadn't been surprised when she offered him the job within minutes of completing the tour of the barn and her house.

It was incredible how much alike they thought. At first when he had pored over the brochures of bathroom fixtures and kitchen cabinets she brought home, it was to give her his opinion on construction and installation. Then it became a game—which one would you pick? The game had acquired a disturbing edge to it when he realized how often their choices matched.

Georgia had to realize it too. There was no way a woman as smart as she was couldn't have. He had begun to wonder what else they might be so compatible about besides glass-front cabinets and floor patterns.

It didn't matter how many lectures he had given himself, his thoughts about Georgia always ran in the same direction. A totally unprofessional direction. That afternoon had been the worst. He had once again been disturbed by how they had chosen the same paint color. There were sixty colors there; how could he have picked the exact same shade she had? He had been trying to shake the sensation by reading the strange names the paint company had given each color, when the name under a pale peach shade caught his eye. *Dawn over Georgia*. He knew the name referred to the state Georgia, not a woman, and it made perfect sense to connect Georgia and peaches. Still his mind had gone in a completely different direction.

He had started to wonder if that pale peach color matched Georgia's skin. The skin he'd never seen, that is. He knew her legs, arms, and face were lightly tanned. His overactive imagination had centered on the pale skin that hadn't been exposed to the summer sun. He had envisioned Georgia lying naked, sleepy-eyed, and totally satisfied across his bed as the first rays of morning light seeped into the room. Desire had hardened his body to the point of aching as he pictured his own version of Dawn over Georgia.

Levi pulled his mind away from such dangerous and foolhardy thoughts and hastily stood up. The late summer afternoon had gotten abnormally hot. Damn the woman and the unnatural power she seemed to have over him. He would rather face a room full of sullen teenagers than that petite blonde with china blue eyes. With a muffled curse, directed solely at himself, he headed inside the house to see what Shane liked on his pizza.

THREE

Four days later Georgia couldn't stand the tension within her own home. The amazing part was, she lived alone! Her carpenter, though, was worrying her to the point that she was about to cross the line in their professional relationship. Levi wasn't going to appreciate her concern, but that morning the man had actually growled at her when she handed him a cup of freshly brewed coffee. She was amazed he hadn't bitten her hand too.

Whatever was wrong with Levi seemed to be eating him from the inside out. He looked as if he hadn't slept in days. She was scared to death that he was ill and was afraid to tell her or seek medical help. She hadn't noticed any rattling coughs, fever bright eyes, or chalky pallor. He just appeared more exhausted with each passing day. He showed up every morning at six-thirty and left dragging his feet at five. He didn't speak unless spoken to first, and then he only talked about the work he was doing.

There had been no more smiles.

That afternoon, as soon as the men laying her kitchen floor packed their truck and left, she was going to sit down with Levi and have a heart-to-heart with him. She didn't think he could go on like this much longer. She knew she couldn't.

The low rumbling of male voices and the closing of the patio screen door signaled the departure of the linoleum installers. Levi was alone in the kitchen and as the saying went, there was no time like the present.

She walked into the room and quickly glanced at the floor, now that it was complete. She had been sneaking peeks all afternoon and had been pleased, both with her choice of the country print that resembled an Amish quilt pattern and the way the men had been installing it. The kitchen was turning out wonderfully and Levi was doing a remarkable job. She only prayed that whatever was bothering him, he wasn't so distressed that he left before completing the shop. She wanted the same miraculous detail carried over into her antique store.

Her gaze fell on the broad shoulders of the man she had come to talk to. He had his back to her and was kneeling in front of an electrical outlet. She shifted to the right and watched enthralled as he spliced the colored wires into the receptacle. He had the sure touch of a man who'd worked with his hands all his life. He had the hands of a carpenter. His fingers were strong, calluses marked his toughened palms, and his wrists were thick and powerful.

He had the hands of a lover.

In her dreams she had felt his hands caress her body, taking her to heights she'd never thought possible. In her dreams he taught her the meaning of desire and passion. In her dreams, anything was possible. Reality was another story.

In reality men wanted her for only one reason, the De Witt bankroll. She'd be the first to admit it was an impressive bankroll, thanks mainly to her brother's hard work over the past sixteen years. It wasn't her bankroll, it was Morgan's. What little money she considered her own was tied up in the antique business and in her new home. She preferred it that way. She was a self-supporting woman who wasn't struggling to get by, but she wasn't rolling in the green stuff either.

From what she knew about Levi, he was a self-supporting man too. He had started his business eight years earlier and had been doing extremely well ever since.

He must have felt her stare because he turned his head and glanced up at her. "Like it?"

She was tempted to tell him that no, she wasn't happy with what she was seeing; that he looked like hell. But she knew he was referring to the newly laid floor. She stepped farther into the room and strolled down the hall to where the powder room and laundry room were. Everything looked bright, spacious, and empty. She returned to the kitchen and smiled. "It's just what I envisioned."

"Good." Levi turned back to the outlet. "The cabinets are being delivered first thing tomorrow morning."

So much for a meaningful conversation, she thought. The man was as talkative as a horse. She leaned against the window frame and watched as he screwed the receptacle into the box and attached the plate cover. "Do you like doing this kind of work?"

He gave her a funny look before moving to the next electrical outlet. "If I didn't like it, I wouldn't be doing it."

"I mean, do you like doing it here?"

"Here?" The wire cutters stripped the black plastic coating off a wire. "Here where? This kitchen, the county, the country? What do you mean by *here*?"

"Here, this kitchen." She frowned as he continued to ignore her and strip the white plastic off another wire. "Do you like working for me on this house?"

He shrugged as he wrapped the wire around a screw and tightened it down. "If I hadn't wanted to work on your house I never would have accepted the job." He connected the copper grounding wire, then glanced over his shoulder as if something had just occurred to him. "Is there a problem?"

"Problem?"

"Is there a problem with my work? Aren't you satisfied with it?" He stood up and glanced around the room as if expecting to see some glaring fault.

"No, your work is excellent and I'm extremely satisfied with the progress you're making." She was appalled that he thought she was criticizing his work. "Everything is wonderful." Lord, what if she'd just insulted him to the point of quitting?

"Well then, what's the problem?" He picked up the plate cover and removed the clear plastic wrap.

"Who said there was a problem?" Maybe she should have just kept her mouth closed and pretended she didn't notice his zombielike appearance.

"My first after-school job," he said, "was shoveling out the stables of a riding academy. It wasn't the most pleasant job for a sixteen-year-old, and I'm sorry to say I didn't give them one hundred percent of my time or energy. My boss asked me one day if I was happy there. Foolish youth that I was, I told him the truth and by the next afternoon I was looking for a new job." He gave her a piercing look before bending back down and screwing on the plate cover. "I'm assuming there's a problem somewhere if you're concerned about my happiness."

"This has nothing to do with your work, Levi. I'm very pleased with the bathroom and the way the kitchen is going."

He straightened to his full imposing height. "If this isn't about my work, then what's it about?"

She glanced once again at the dark circles beneath his brown eyes and the exhausted stoop to his shoulders. Two tiny cuts marked his jaw where he had shaved that morning. His forehead was creased by a worried frown, and she wanted to smooth the lines away. This was not the same man she'd met a month ago. Something was drastically wrong, and that gave her the strength to voice her concern. "It's about your health, Levi." She flinched at his startled expression. "No offense, but you're beginning to look like hell." He wasn't *beginning* to look like hell, he *did* look like hell.

Levi blinked several times before muttering, "I look like hell?"

"Well, not exactly hell." Decorum was such a terrible quality at times. "I was just wondering if the job was becoming too much for you to handle."

"Too much?" His voice thundered in the empty room.

"I meant too much for one man, Levi. This wasn't just a simple kitchen remodeling job. One of the contractors I contacted advised me to rip down the entire house and build a nice two-story colonial on the spot." She shuddered at the thought of destroying the house. Sometime in the fifties the kitchen had been remodeled, so it wasn't as if Levi had destroyed the past when he gutted that entire room.

"You've been working long hours, six days a week, and you look exhausted. You aren't the most social person I've ever met, but this morning I actually had to count my fingers after you snatched the coffee cup out of my hand. Something is bothering you and I'm concerned." She glanced at him and swallowed nervously. He looked ready to explode. His jaw was clenched and a vein in his forehead throbbed wildly. Instinct told her she was looking at a stick of dynamite and it was lit. "Is there anything I can do?" she finished in a whisper.

"You're concerned about me!" He stared at her as if she had just slithered out from underneath a rock and he wasn't sure what species she was. "My mother lives in Christiana and I was married once. I'm not in the market for another wife or someone who worries about me."

She cringed. The last thing she had wanted was Levi getting the idea she was applying for the position of his "significant other." Lord, this wasn't turning out as she'd planned. "Well, I was almost married once myself and I wasn't applying for the position of your keeper. I was just trying to be friendly by expressing my concern for your well-being." She could feel the tide of embarrassment flooding its way up her cheeks and prayed her face didn't appear as hot as it felt.

"What do you mean *almost* married? The institution of matrimony isn't like horseshoes. Either you were married or you weren't. Leaners don't count."

"The marriage was called off a month before the wedding. So no, I wasn't married, but that doesn't mean I can't be concerned for a fellow human being. I was simply—"

"Who called off the wedding?"

She was thrown off balance by his abrupt question. "What does it matter who called off the wedding?" She wasn't about to tell Levi she had been jilted while trying on her wedding gown.

"You had to be the one who called off the wedding." Levi's hard glare pierced her heart.

"Me?"

"What was the matter? Wasn't he rich enough for you?"

The heat flooding her face turned to ice. Was that what Levi thought? That she picked prospective bridegrooms by their bank balance? How little he knew. She sadly shook her head. "No, Adam was the one who called off the wedding." She glanced out the patio door, noticing the way the late afternoon sunlight filtered through the large maple tree. "He met someone else and fell in love. They're getting married next week."

She still couldn't believe Adam Young was marrying his lost Emily and becoming stepfather to her three children. Children! Who would have thought Adam would want the little tykes and, if his story could be believed, an old rambling Queen Anne house and half the Bronx zoo. Two weeks earlier, at an estate sale, she had found the perfect wedding present for Adam and Emily. It was a gilded birdcage large enough to hold a small ostrich. She had a certain macaw in mind. For some reason she was positive it would fit right into the new Young family.

Adam was getting married and she was still alone. She didn't begrudge Adam his happiness, but it still hurt her when she thought about him. Why hadn't he wanted her? What was wrong with her?

She could feel the tears pool in her eyes and clog her throat. She refused to turn around and look at Levi. All of a sudden Mister Don't Be Concerned for Me was awfully quiet. She couldn't face him right now. "If you'll excuse me I have something I need to check on." She cleared her throat and opened the patio door. "I'm sorry if I embarrassed you with my concern, Levi. It won't happen again." She stepped out onto the porch, closed the screen door behind her, and headed for the barn.

Levi watched Georgia walk away and cursed every four-letter word he knew under his breath. He felt like the world's biggest first-class jerk. He had hurt her. He had heard the tears in her voice and known by the way she refused to turn around that there were tears in her eyes as well. He wasn't sure if it had been his hateful comment about her preferring a rich husband or the memories of her ex-fiancé that had caused the pain. It didn't really matter. Either way he was at fault.

What in the world had gotten into him? He had never been so nasty to another person in his entire life. Georgia had been honestly concerned for his health, and he'd acted as if she were shoving her nose where it didn't belong. He had a mirror at home. He faced it every morning and he knew what Georgia had been talking about. He looked like hell.

Stress and lack of sleep could do that to a person. Shane had him tied up into so many knots he could no longer see the end of the rope. Sunday he had taken the boy to his parents' house, down in Christiana, for a family barbecue. A dozen cousins had shown up to welcome Shane to the area and to let the boy know he had family. Shane's merely being disrespectful would have been an improvement over the way he'd acted. When the boy wasn't glaring at someone, he was ignoring them all. Levi's mother had ended up in the kitchen crying and demanding to know what had happened to her grandson. How could her sweet Caroline rest in heaven when her son was having such a difficult time on earth? The men had shaken their heads and wondered about God's strange ways.

Tears weren't going to help his nephew and shaking one's head never solved a thing. Levi was on his own where Shane was concerned. And he'd never felt more helpless in his life. He didn't have the answers. Hell, he wasn't even sure he knew all the questions.

He had tried talking to Shane. The boy either ignored him or told him, in no uncertain terms, where to go. He had tried yelling. He had tried revoking privileges. He had even gone as far as offering Shane twenty bucks if he just wore a plain T-shirt and jeans to the family barbecue. Shane had told him where he could stick his twenty bucks and ended up wearing a pair of jeans that drunks sleeping in rat-infested alleys wouldn't have been caught dead in, and a T-shirt that portrayed a rock band with painted faces, spiked hair, and a boa constrictor wrapped around the lead singer's throat. Short of holding the boy down and changing him himself, there hadn't been a whole lot Levi could do about the situation besides canceling the cookout. He couldn't have done that. His parents had been anxiously waiting to see Shane, ever since he called to let them know he was taking in the boy.

He should have canceled the outing. The day had been a total disaster, and the strain between Shane and himself had been stretched even tighter. Sleep was a luxury that had been sacrificed to worry, and it was showing. Now Georgia had picked up on it, and his own mother had made a comment or two on Sunday. Fatherhood obviously didn't agree with him.

Something had to give with Shane, and give soon. Levi only prayed it wasn't his sanity.

It was still no reason to take out his frustration on Georgia. The woman was too nice for her own good, and he'd gone and stepped all over her sweetness. The Lord knew there wasn't an abundance of people who cared enough about their fellow man. He owed her an apology. A big apology.

He unbuckled his tool belt and lowered it carefully to the floor, then followed Georgia out to the barn. The afternoon sun heated his face and arms. His chambray shirt clung to his back, but he ignored the heat. Summer's heat never bothered him. He'd rather work when it was one hundred degrees than when it was twenty degrees with a foot of snow on the ground.

The sliding doors were wide open, allowing brilliant sunlight to spill into the barn. He stood by the door and watched Georgia as she polished an antique birdcage to a gleaming glow. He'd noticed the gilded cage the week before, but hadn't thought much about it. Now he wondered what she planned to do with the thing. It looked large enough to hold a child.

That morning Georgia had left the house in what he classed as her "shopkeeper's attire"—a flowing skirt, silky blouse, and low-heeled sandals that did incredible things for her ankles. She had returned late in the afternoon and had changed into a pair of navy shorts and a white T-shirt with tiny ships all over it. The shirt should have looked ridiculous on a grown woman. So why did he have this sudden urge to whistle like Popeye and shout, "Well, blow me down!"?

Georgia appeared to have gotten herself under control. There were no tears that he could see, no sobs. The woman had class, he had to give her that. He'd like to give her a lot more, but common sense told him otherwise. Georgia De Witt was definitely not the woman for him, even if he were interested in a relationship, which he most definitely was not. Add a newly acquired "son" named Seaweed and the odds of his forming any relationship at all were nil.

His gaze traveled up the length of her lightly tanned legs to her gorgeously curved bottom. A man could feast his gaze on her all day long and never grow tired of the view. How could her fiancé have fallen in love with another woman? That seemed like the bigger impossibility.

There was some idiot out there who had actually won Georgia's love and her agreement to become his wife, and then threw it all away. The man had to have gerbil food for brains.

Georgia moved to the other side of the cage and noticed him standing there. The white polishing cloth stilled. "Yes, Levi, is there something I can do for you?"

He marveled at the calmness in her voice. She acted as if they were holding a conversation at the local country club instead of inside a run-down barn. He stepped into the cool interior. "Yes, there is." He walked closer to her and the cage. "You can accept my apology. My comment about you breaking your engagement because the bridegroom wasn't rich enough was uncalled for and totally unwarranted."

She gave a slight nod. "Apology accepted." She turned and went back to running the cloth up and down each small bar of the cage.

He went on. "You never did or said anything that would lead me to believe you would only marry a man for his money." He glanced around the barn and envisioned it as Georgia's antique shop. "I would have to make a guess and say you wouldn't need a man's money to get by on. You're a highly intelligent and successful businesswoman."

"Drop it, Levi. I already accepted your apology." She frowned at the cage, still buffing the bars to a high gloss.

He watched the slow, steady movements of the rag. "There is one thing that's bothering me, Georgia. I find it hard to believe that some man named Adam left you for another woman a month before your wedding."

"What's so hard to understand? He met another woman, fell in love, and wanted out. No complicated logic there."

"Is this guy mentally incompetent?"

Georgia gave a throaty laugh. "Adam Young is anything but incompetent. He's the brilliant architect who designed the Lavender Hall Estates."

A low whistle escaped Levi's lips before he could stop it. There wasn't a soul within the tristate area who hadn't heard of the Lavender Hall Estates. Georgia had been engaged to the man who had designed it all! Talk about a perfect match. "The man still has to be a moron, Georgia. Who in his right mind could even look at another woman when he had you?"

"A man who didn't love me." She bit her lower lip and crushed the cloth in her hand. "A man who didn't find me desirable."

Levi felt his heart lurch against his rib cage. It was becoming a little clearer now. Unbelievable, but clearer. Georgia thought she was undesirable. "It must have been difficult for him to design those estates when he's totally blind."

Georgia gave him a ghost of a smile that instead of lightening his heart, pulled at it more. Her smile never reached her eyes. "That's awfully sweet of you, Levi. But I learned a long time ago what men see when they look at me."

He stepped closer. Close enough to spot the vulnerability in her blue eyes. "What do men see when they look at you, Georgia?"

It took her a moment to decide if she wanted

to answer him, but she did. "They see the De Witt fortune."

He smiled as he glanced around the empty barn. If cobwebs were spun out of gold, then she would indeed be a wealthy woman. "I didn't realize the antique business was that good." Any man who looked at Georgia and saw dollar signs was indeed a fool.

"There is money."

He shook his head and took another step closer. "There can't be that much, Georgia. You're a very beautiful and desirable woman. I can't imagine there's a man alive who looks at you and thinks about money."

"There have been several." She glanced away from him and studied the toes of her dusty sneakers. "I'm not the type of woman who inspires gut-wrenching desire, Levi. I'm a cool, level-headed businesswoman."

"I can't dispute that, but you're also a very attractive woman." He loved the way her blush swept up her cheeks. How could a thirty-two-year-old woman be so sweetly innocent?

She shook her head, not looking up.

He cupped her chin and forced her to look at him. "Do you know what I see when I look at you?"

"What?"

"I see the afternoon sky in your eyes." His thumb stroked her cheek. "I hear the morning breeze in your voice." The pad of his thumb rubbed across her lower lip as a kitteny purr vibrated in the back of her throat. Desire rushed to his groin. "I feel the heat of your passion whenever we're close."

She swayed toward him. "You do?"

The slight redness of her lower lip, where she had bitten it, was too much for him. He had to taste Georgia, just once in his life. "I see all that, and much, much more." He lowered his head and claimed her mouth.

Desire ripped through his body as she raised her arms and twined them around his neck. The soft little purr emerged from her mouth and he greedily snatched it up. He had only wanted to taste her sweetness, but as she pressed her breasts against his chest and deepened the kiss, he devoured her with his mouth. He couldn't get enough. He needed more. Wanted more.

Her fingers wove into his hair and pressed him closer. Her tongue matched his, stroke for stroke and thrust for thrust. Her purrs turned into moans and he answered each one of them. His hands cupped her bottom and pressed her soft womanly curves against his bulging jeans.

Her willingness to accept and participate in the explosion of heat that had erupted between them brought him back to his senses. This was Georgia De Witt in his arms! Within a minute they would be ripping off each other's clothes and going at it on a filthy barn floor. Where were his senses? And he wasn't referring to the mass of sensations centered below his belt buckle.

He hastily broke the kiss and pushed Georgia an arm's length away. She looked as dazed and confused as he felt. She also appeared as excited. Lord, temptation was only inches away. Her eyes were bright and shiny, and her mouth had the appearance of just being thoroughly kissed. She looked incredibly sexy wearing his kiss.

He dropped his hands and ran his fingers through his hair. "I'm sorry, I shouldn't have done that. That won't happen again, Georgia." He took a step back.

She touched one finger to her mouth in wonder. "It won't?"

"No." He took another step back, toward the open doors. He had to get out of there before he did something incredibly stupid, like kiss her again. "There is one thing I want you to know, Georgia."

"What's that?" She didn't follow him toward the door, and for that he was extremely thankful.

"The entire time I was kissing you, I never once thought about money." He turned quickly and headed back for the relative safety of the house. He hoped his impromptu lesson in teaching Georgia how desirable she was had worked, because he was paying a heavy price. His gut was telling him he was going to pay that price for a long time to come.

FOUR

Georgia paced the length of her living room for what seemed like the hundredth time. In reality it was probably only her ninety-fifth time. Levi was late! It was already way past eight o'clock, and she had managed to go through the entire pot of coffee by herself. The burning sensation in her stomach was telling her that she really ought to think about cutting down on caffeine.

She walked to the window and watched as a yellow school bus made its way down the road. It was only the last week of August and already the kids were back in school. When she went to school, they didn't start back until sometime after Labor Day. It seemed like a lifetime ago that she had boarded her first school bus and waved goodbye to her teary-eyed mom. She turned away from the window as the red taillights and big yellow rear door disappeared from view.

The need to keep moving sent her through the kitchen. It was nearly completed. For the past two days, ever since the kiss, Levi had been a man obsessed with finishing the house. The powder room was done except for a cabinet above the commode. She had spent part of the previous night hanging a curtain and setting out towels and a basket overflowing with fancy soaps. Levi had reconnected her washer and dryer before leaving the previous night, and she had done a couple loads of laundry. In the kitchen, all the cabinets were in, along with the cooktop and built-in oven. The refrigerator had been moved into place and the sink connected. The room had turned out exactly as she had envisioned it. Levi had about one more day's worth of work, then he'd be clear to start on the barn. She wasn't sure if he had pushed himself so hard because he was eager to get on with the barn or if he just wanted to work away from her.

For two days he had been avoiding her as if she had some highly contagious disease that could be transmitted by sight alone. She had discovered a message on her answering machine that morning when she got out of the shower, and it was the longest conversation Levi had held with her since that afternoon in the barn. It was a whole two sentences. *Something came up. I'm going to be late.*

Since quarter after six that morning she had been wondering what that *something* was. The other day in the barn she'd known what had come up, and it hadn't been all her blood pressure and heart rate. Levi had wanted her! And he hadn't been happy about it at all.

She had found a man whose kisses could scorch the polish right off her toenails, and he vowed never to do it again! Well, wasn't life just grand? The mere memory of the heat from his kiss could set butterflies frolicing in her stomach once again, and all he seemed to want to do was forget their embrace had ever happened. She wasn't willing to forget it or to allow him to forget that he had been the one to pull her into his arms and kiss two years off her life. He had started this frustration. By the Saints, he should satisfy it.

She just wasn't sure how to convey her interest, or her determination, to a man like Levi.

Her dates, the men she was normally attracted to, were usually suit-and-tie wearing individuals, without a callus or blister in sight. She knew how to handle that kind of man, knew what he expected from a woman he was dating. Levi was in a completely different ball park from the high-browed society she was used to mingling with. A ball park she had only glimpsed from the outside. She wondered what a ticket to enter would cost her.

The sound of Levi's truck pulling up her gravel drive sent her hurrying to the window. She watched as Levi got out of the driver's side and apparently argued with someone who was sitting in the passenger seat. The shadowy silhouette shook its head a couple of times. Levi spoke some more. Eventually the passenger door opened, and she quickly backed away from the window before they spotted her spying. Whoever it was, she was going to be meeting him or her soon.

A minute later, Levi was knocking in his customary fashion on the front door. She smoothed her hands down the sides of her celery-colored skirt and gave the hem of her sleeveless white blouse a smart tug. She had two business appointments later that morning and had dressed appropriately. The suit she had chosen was both professional and attractive, yet her brother had questioned her taste when she had worn it to lunch a month ago. It seemed her brother hadn't approved of the way some of the other male patrons had stared at her throughout the meal. The suit had been a great confidence builder, even though she hadn't worn it since then. Today had seemed like a great opportunity to wear it again. She wanted to gauge Levi's reaction to it.

She opened the front door with her best welcoming smile. Years of proper training had to be relied on to keep that smile from fading. Levi was his same heart-stopping self. His companion was a totally different matter. The boy looked as if he could use an hour in a barber's chair and six months on a therapist's couch.

"Ms. De Witt," Levi said, "I would like to introduce you to my nephew, Shane Weaver."

Nephew! Levi was related to this scowling, dog-collar-wearing teenager? She forced her smile to brighten as she held out her hand. "Hello, Shane."

The boy ignored her hand. "The name's Seaweed."

"Seaweed?" She couldn't have heard him right. She had to have misunderstood what he had said.

"My nephew prefers to be called by that ridiculous name, which I refuse to do." Levi glared at his nephew. "Shane came to live with me about two weeks ago. I'm his legal guardian now."

Georgia caught the glimpse of pain in Shane's eyes before he masked it with belligerence. Her smile softened as she backed away from the door, so they could enter. "Come on in, Seaweed." She gave Levi a quick glance as he continued to stand there. "You can come in too."

Shane gave his uncle a contemptuous smile as he followed her into the living room.

Levi stepped into the room and closed the door behind them. "It seems my nephew has an aversion to rules and regulations. Late yesterday afternoon he managed to get himself suspended from school. This morning I had an eight o'clock appointment with the vice principal to discuss the matter. *Shane*, here, attended the meeting and managed to turn a three-day in-school suspension into a five-day out-of-school suspension."

She glanced at the boy, who, if his smile could

be believed, seemed quite pleased with this development. "Oh, my!" She had never so much as received a reprimand or detention, let alone been suspended. Her parents or Morgan would have crucified her.

"Not exactly my words, but you get the picture," Levi said. "I can't very well leave him at home during the day while I work here. With your permission I would like to hire him on, at my expense, of course, to work here for the next five days. Maybe some hard physical labor will knock some sense into him."

"What about his studies?"

"During lunch I can run to school and pick up his assignments. He can complete any work he's missing at night after we get home."

She turned to Shane and tried to gauge his reaction to his uncle's suggestion of working there. If her instincts were on the mark, he wasn't too happy with the proposal. But what did her instincts know? As far as she could figure, she didn't possess one maternal instinct in her whole body. She had always classed child rearing in the same category as car engines and figuring out her taxes: better left to the experts. Right now, Levi was the expert. He was, after all, the boy's guardian and uncle. If he thought some physical work would be good for the boy, who was she to argue? "As long as he does his studies at night and it's safe, I don't have a problem with him working here."

"Good." Levi kept his gaze on his nephew. "You don't mind if he starts this morning, do you?"

"Of course not." She gave Shane a friendly smile. The boy would be handsome if he had a normal haircut, decent clothes, and if he nixed the jewelry. Perky cheerleaders with bouncy ponytails and short skirts would be falling at his feet. She could see a resemblance to Levi in his strong jaw and height. The boy looked to be sixteen, and already he was pushing the six-foot mark. "Would you like something to drink or eat, Seaweed?" She hid her cringe at saying his nickname. If her memory served her correctly, individuality was very important to teenagers. "I have some orange juice and I think some blueberry bagels."

"Cool." The boy smiled.

"I really don't think that's such a—"

"Good," Georgia snapped, cutting Levi off midsentence. "Don't think for once." Shane's smile was identical to the one Levi had flashed at her days before. "He's a growing boy, Levi. The way you've been scowling at him all morning I bet he didn't get a chance for a decent breakfast at home. What's five more minutes anyway?"

She didn't bother to look at Levi or at Shane as she headed out of the room and into the kitchen. For the life of her she couldn't figure out why she had just invited Levi's nephew to stay for a quick bite to eat. The flash of pain she had seen in his eyes and the too rebellious way of dressing tugged at her heartstrings. Under normal circumstances she never would have snapped at Levi like that, but who said these were normal circumstances? She had never been kissed like that before, and the sleep she was losing just thinking about it was making her cranky. She had every right to snap at the thick-headed man.

"Wow, Unc, why didn't you tell me your boss was a major babe-o-rama?" Shane followed Georgia out of the room like a lamb who'd just found Bo Peep.

Levi stood there stunned. *Babe-o-rama!* Shane thought Georgia was a major babe-o-rama! Lord help him, he was going to be out of his mind by the end of the day. He couldn't handle both Shane and Georgia at the same time. This was a mistake, a big mistake. It had to be. The first sign of insanity setting in had to be his thinking of employing his nephew to work on Georgia's antique shop. The boy knew nothing about carpentry, and obviously less about women. No one looking at Georgia would class her as "babe-o-rama" material. The woman wore class the way most women wore clothes.

He didn't want to think about clothes, especially Georgia's. She had looked gorgeous and delectable when she opened the door. Not a damn thing new with that. Except this morning she was dressed in a pale green skirt that hugged her hips and a blouse that clung to her breasts as if it had been custom-made for them. The enticing view of her swaying hips as she left the room had driven up his blood pressure fifty points. His nephew's crude comment had driven it up another fifty. He could only pray that Georgia hadn't heard the comment or that she would accept his apology on his nephew's behalf.

Shane never should have made such a disrespectful remark. Then again, his nephew shouldn't have told the vice principal what he thought about her views on appropriate school attire. It seemed his bare-breasted mermaid earring violated some dress code. The day before, the first day of school, he had refused to remove the dangling earring and received the three-day suspension. That morning Levi had hoped Shane would apologize and remove the offending piece of jewelry. He had not. Instead he had told the vice principal what she could do with her rules and had received the five-day out-of-school suspension.

Levi personally thought a bar of soap and a good paddling was what the boy needed, not more time at home. But short of holding him down and yanking the earring from his ear, there wasn't a whole lot Levi could do. Shane had to learn to be responsible for his own actions. Maybe suspension sounded cool to the teen now, but Levi could guarantee that after five days of working for him, Shane would be changing his tune and removing the earring. Eleventh grade was going to look awfully easy after what Levi planned to put him through. And having breakfast with a major babe-o-rama wasn't on the schedule.

He stepped into the kitchen and glared at Shane. The boy was holding a tall glass of orange juice and laughing at something Georgia had just said. He had absolutely no right to appear so darn happy after the morning of humiliation Levi had just gone through.

And Georgia! He didn't even want to think about Georgia. He had been trying desperately not to think about Georgia for days. Or the way she tasted. Or the funny little purr that had rumbled in the back of her throat when they had kissed. Or the way her hips had seemed to fit so perfectly against his. He especially didn't want to think about the way her nipples had beaded beneath her shirt as she pressed up against his chest. The woman was a phantom who stole into his every dream and made him ache until dawn.

Standing in front of him with that tight green skirt and her blond hair piled on top of her head, just begging to be released from whatever was holding it up, was making him ache all over again. Lately, the ache wasn't going away. It was a constant pulsing reminder of things he couldn't have. Things he never should have been tempted to taste in the first place.

He turned to his nephew and gave the boy the sharp side of his tongue. "We're not here to socialize, Shane. We're here to work." He turned toward the patio doors. "Thank Ms. De Witt for the juice and let's go. Because of your little stunt at school I'm already an hour and a half behind."

Levi ignored Georgia's murderous glare as his nephew downed the remaining orange juice and wiped his mouth with the back of his hand. Shane gave Georgia a huge grin. "Thanks, George, that really hit the spot."

"You're welcome, Seaweed." Her scowl toward Levi slipped into a smile for the boy. "We'll do bagels some other time when your uncle's in a better mood."

Georgia raised her eyebrows at him and gave him such a sugary-sweet smile it nearly made him gag. "Maybe he's in such a terrible mood because he didn't get his usual morning cup of coffee. Would you like me to put on a fresh pot, Levi?"

"*Touché.*" Her barb struck with piercing accuracy. He usually got a morning cup of coffee from her pot. But it was an entirely different situation with Shane. The boy was being put to work as a form of punishment. He didn't know what else to do with Shane. What did other parents do? He couldn't very well beat the boy. His own parents had used the standard grounding punishment, which was an excellent deterrent, except Shane hadn't made any friends yet, so he hadn't asked to go out anywhere. Levi had been hoping that once school started Shane would make some friends and begin acting like a normal teen. Now for the first time, and since he'd witnessed the other high school students hurrying to their classes that morning, he had to wonder what a normal teen acted like nowadays. His own youth seemed to be a long way in his past, and he was beginning to feel every one of those years.

"Come on, Shane, Ms. De Witt has work to do." He opened the patio doors and stepped out onto the porch without looking at Georgia. He didn't want to see her lovely face squinch up in anger at the way he was treating his nephew. He already knew he was rapidly becoming a failure as far as Shane was concerned. As soon as his nephew joined him on the porch and closed the door behind them, he headed for the barn with the boy in tow.

Georgia kicked off her high heels the instant she stepped into the kitchen. She draped her suit jacket over the back of a chair, tossed her purse and briefcase onto the table, and headed for the refrigerator and an ice-cold drink of anything. The afternoon had turned out to be a real scorcher. Thankfully, summer was nearing its close, and by the end of next month the new heat and central air system she was having installed would be up and running.

She grabbed the first can of diet soda she could reach, popped the top, and took a deep drink. Heaven was a cold drink on a hot day. She satisfied her initial thirst, then took a quick tour of the rooms to see if Levi had finished. The original oak and glass cabinets, which had been in the kitchen when she bought the house, were now hanging in the laundry room and the powder room. Levi had stripped them down to the original wood and varnished them to a gleaming glossy finish. They looked wonderful. All they needed now was for her to hang curtains on the inside of the glass to hide the clutter from view. Fancy china or even neatly arranged everyday dishes were one thing; plastic bottles of laundry detergent, rolls of toilet paper, and assorted bottles of medicine were a totally different story. She walked around the kitchen and noticed that Levi also had given the window trim its second coat of paint. He was finished with the inside of her house.

She didn't know how she felt about it. That was the strange part. The kitchen and master bathroom were wonderful, exactly as she had envisioned them to be. She was thrilled and truly excited to know he would now be starting to turn the barn into her dream store. So why did she feel so disappointed that she wouldn't be tripping over him daily throughout her house? He'd only be a hundred yards away, and yet she missed him. It seemed impossible. It definitely was strange. And it was downright frightening.

She left the empty soda can on the counter and headed upstairs to change. She wanted to see what progress Levi and his nephew had made in the barn, and teetering around on uneven plank flooring wearing high heels was asking for trouble. Being laid up with a broken leg for six weeks or so wasn't on her schedule.

She slipped out of the skirt and blouse and quickly stripped off the pantyhose. The windows were all opened, but not a breeze stirred the lacy curtains. She could hear some distant pounding coming from the barn. Whatever they were doing in there at least sounded impressive. She pulled on a pair of shorts and a sleeveless top before taking off her jewelry and dropping the earrings, watch, and necklace into the crystal dish on top of her bureau. Drawing the curtain aside, she glanced out toward the barn. Most of her view was obscured by the massive maple that stood between the house and the barn, but she could see a good portion of the barn. She couldn't see Levi.

Levi was the legal guardian of his nephew. Somehow, especially after meeting Shane, she was still having a hard time picturing it. Levi and Shane were nothing alike! Then again, she had to guess most adults didn't look anything like their teenage sons or daughters, or else the world would be one very strange-looking place indeed. She had missed the wild hippie, flower child era by at least a decade, and she had been too old for the designer era of the eighties. She had spent her rebellious youth dressed in jeans, sneakers, and comfortable sweatshirts.

Today's youth seemed to go for shock value in their attire. Tops of boxer underwear showed above baggy jeans all over the place. Girls and boys pierced their ears, once, twice, and three times. If that failed to appall parents, they pierced their tongues, eyebrows, navals, and Lord only knew what other body parts. Tattoos were big, as well, as was strange-colored hair.

Poor Levi, he must have his hands full with Shane, or rather, Seaweed. Seaweed! What kind of name was that for a sixteen-year-old? The boy obviously thought it was cool, or he wouldn't be insisting everyone use it. Levi was stubborn enough not to honor the boy's wishes. On the one hand, she could see why he refused to call his nephew a name that made her think of slimy, foul-smelling algae. But she had seen the pain in the boy's eyes and had respected his wishes. She knew Levi didn't approve of her calling the boy by his nickname, but Shane's hurt had touched her heart.

She had so many questions about Shane. Why did Levi have custody of the boy? Where were his parents? Had something happened to them? Lord, she prayed not. Had his parents thrown up their hands in disgust with his appearance and attitude and just handed him over to Levi? She hoped that hadn't happened either. That, in a way, would be worse than losing one's parents. To actually have parents who no longer wanted you! She didn't know what to think. She only knew Levi wasn't as single and free as she had thought. He had a child. A sixteen-year-old who wore a bigger dog collar than Lassie's and whose hairdo was a reject from the movie *The Last of the Mohicans*.

Georgia released the curtain and turned away from the view. No wonder Levi had been acting moody and looked so exhausted. The man must be going out of his mind trying to deal with Shane. Poor Levi. She remembered the pain in the boy's eyes and sighed as she left the room. Poor Shane.

Ten minutes later she stood at the entrance of the barn clasping a tray of ice-cold drinks and shuddering as she glanced around. She had thought the empty, hay-strewn, cobweb infested barn had looked bad. It was nothing compared with what it looked like now. There was still dried hay all around and the cobwebs seemed to get bigger every day, but Levi and Shane were busy knocking down walls and dust was flying everywhere. The men seemed to be trying to outdo each other with the force of their swings. Levi was naturally winning, but Shane was holding his own. They had both removed their shirts, and she could see perspiration clinging to Shane's shoulders and arms.

Levi's chest was another matter. The man had a chest that could stop Hollywood in its filmmaking tracks. Lord save her sanity and her rioting hormones. The temperature inside the barn had shot up twenty degrees! Her breath lodged somewhere deep in her windpipe, and she couldn't have swallowed if someone had held champagne to her lips. The tray trembled and ice cubes clanked against the sides of the glasses. She'd known Levi had a marvelous build, but to see him half naked was . . . It took her a moment before she could come up with a word that described her feelings, and the only one that covered them all was "stimulating". Levi was stimulating!

She stepped into the shadows of the barn, out of the direct light of the doorway. She wanted to appreciate the view for a bit longer. Hell, if she was going to be truthful, she wanted time to pull herself together so Levi didn't see her drooling at the sight of his naked chest. Years of hard physical work had honed that chest to perfection. Shoulders broad enough to carry half the world gleamed a golden bronze under the shaft of light filtering through the open hayloft door. His pecs and biceps were hard rocks of muscles, and a soft covering of brown curls blanketed his chest and drew her gaze downward to where the hair arrowed into the waistband of his jeans. Levi didn't need any fancy belts or flashy big buckles to draw her attention there. It came naturally. Like breathing. Breathing heavily.

He swung his powerful arms, and the sledgehammer once again crashed into the wooden wall that had been constructed between two stalls. The twelve-inch-wide board gave up its fight and flew against the opposite wall, then clattered to the floor to join the other boards Levi and Shane had broken free. She knew it was in Levi's plans to reuse the aged lumber when he constructed her shop. She just hoped the wood would hold together that long. Levi and Shane both seemed determined to take out their frustrations on the innocent wood.

She stepped farther into the barn and called, "Anyone ready for a break?"

The sledgehammer in Levi's grasp faltered slightly at her voice and connected with the wall off its original mark. The sound of splintering wood filled the barn.

Shane chuckled, dropped his sledgehammer, and headed toward her. "Miss, Unc?"

Levi scowled at the piece of lumber that had splintered. He took two more whacks with the sledge and added the pieces to the already large pile.

Shane reached for a frosty glass. "Thanks, George. This is great. Unc promised me a break half an hour ago."

Levi grabbed his shirt, which had been hanging on a nail near the door, and slipped it on. He buttoned four buttons before making his way toward them. "It was five minutes ago, not thirty."

Georgia couldn't prevent the disappointment that swamped her at his old-fashioned act of courtesy, putting on his shirt in front of a lady. She wanted a closer look at his chest, but was half relieved that he had donned the shirt. If paralysis had almost overcome her when she was twenty feet away from him, she couldn't imagine what she would have done if he had stood shirtless directly in front of her. Probably stammer, most definitely blush, and assuredly beg. Her gaze was riveted to the deep V at the neck of his shirt, where a few dark curls peeked over the soft material.

Levi stopped directly in front of her and stood perfectly still until she raised her gaze. A hungry look filled his dark brown eyes. A look that said he had been without a meal for a very long time.

She held his gaze with what she considered a great deal of courage, considering she was beginning to feel like a pork chop and he was a starving wolf. "It's iced tea. Not homemade, but it comes from the best carton in town."

Levi reached for the glass without breaking eye contact. "Thanks." He took a long drink, nearly emptying the glass before glancing at his nephew who had watched their exchange with a great deal of interest. "Break's over." He handed Georgia the glass and went back to the wall.

Shane finished his drink, placed it on the tray, and watched his uncle walk away. "Boy, and I thought he only had it in for me." He gave her a huge grin that didn't quite mask the tremor that had been in his voice. "What did you do, disagree with him or play your stereo too loud?"

Georgia leaned forward and said, "Worse."

She knew Levi was listening to every word they said.

"What?"

I kissed him! She couldn't very well tell his sixteen-year-old nephew that, but she wanted to. It was the truth. Instead, in an extravagant whisper that Levi could easily overhear, she said, "I put the screwdrivers back in his toolbox in the wrong order."

FIVE

Levi sat on his back deck and listened to the sounds of the night. A faint patch of light fell onto the deck from the patio doors, but other than that he was in complete darkness. He hadn't bothered to turn on the outside lights. Light would be too revealing, and in the mood he was in, he really didn't want anything illuminated, including himself. Especially himself.

He had screwed up royally. Both with Georgia and with Shane. The guilt was festering deep inside him like a cancer. It was eating him up and if he didn't find a way to stop it, it would destroy him.

He never should have put Shane through such a rough day. The boy was totally exhausted and had barely managed to keep his eyes open through dinner. His spiked Mohawk had wilted into a pathetic flap of gelled hair, and as hard as

Shane tried to hide it, Levi knew the boy sported a couple of blisters on his palms. On the way home from Georgia's, Levi had stopped at the little pizza place on Main Street and picked up a couple of steak sandwiches and a bag of chips. Shane had sat at the counter in the kitchen and downed the sandwich in a dozen bites that would have made a sumo wrestler proud. Levi had barely finished half of his own when Shane claimed the shower, then disappeared into his room.

Levi closed his eyes. He could barely detect the music playing in Shane's room. That could mean one of three things. Shane had fallen asleep with the music on low, or he was using his earphones and his hearing really was totally shot, or he had actually gotten tired of listening to his uncle yell about the loud music and had consciously turned it down. The volume of the music hadn't changed during the last hour. That was how long Levi had been sitting out back contemplating the approaching darkness and his messed-up life.

His nephew was amazing, he mused. Shane knew exactly which buttons to press in people and was ruthless in pressing them. Not for the first time he wondered who had taught Shane that disturbing quality, because it surely hadn't been his sister or her husband.

Caroline and Ben had been the two nicest people he had ever known and if their life had lacked anything, it was the inability to have any more children after Shane. Caroline had wanted a house filled with children, but had accepted the news there would be no more with grace and her unshakable belief that it was the Lord's will. Levi didn't know anything about the Lord's will, but he had been damned happy his sister had pulled through giving birth to Shane. That tiny, screaming infant had nearly cost her her life. He would have been happier still if there had never been a fire in the barn that had taken her life and Ben's sixteen years later.

He didn't know how to reach Caroline's son. Ben's brother and his wife, as well as Shane's grandparents, didn't know how either. When he had called the older Weavers the other night, after Shane was in his room, all Lottie Weaver had done was cry and apologize for not warning him about Shane's appearance and behavior. They had been terrified he might not take the boy. In all honesty, he would have thought about it harder, but the result would have been the same. Shane was not only his nephew, but also his second chance at fatherhood. And he was blowing it in spades.

The fragrance of pine trees mingling with the smell of marigolds he had planted around the deck filled his nostrils. He loved summers on top of his little mountain. For that fact, he loved the autumn, winter, and spring too. There was such peace up here, it was almost a tangible thing. He glanced at the room at the end of the house. Shane's room. The curtains were closed against the night, just as they were always closed against the daylight. His heart constricted once again for the boy and his loss.

To lose both parents in such a tragic way was unimaginable, but then to be shuffled from an uncle's home to a grandparents' home and then halfway across the country to another uncle's home only made the situation worse. Especially since it was an uncle he barely knew or saw. Levi didn't know how he was going to reach the boy, but he knew one thing; no matter what, he wasn't shuffling the boy off to another unsuspecting relative. They were in it together for the long haul.

He stood up and stretched the kinks out of his back. He had taken a shower after Shane had, and the pounding hot spray had relieved a lot of the tension in his body, but not his mind. He wasn't a man who explained his actions to anyone, but Georgia deserved a better explanation than the one he had given her that morning about why his nephew was working with him. A person would have to have been blind not to see her stunned expression when she found Shane standing next to him on her doorstep, even though she covered it admirably. The kid was dressed for trouble. Levi would be the first to admit that he didn't like to judge a person by his or her appearance, but if he didn't know Shane, he'd be counting the family silver after the youth left.

He walked into the house and locked the patio door behind him. His next stop was the bathroom where he spent five minutes rooting around in the medicine cabinet until he found what he was looking for; ointment for Shane's blisters.

He knocked softly on Shane's door and was half surprised when the boy answered immediately. "Yeah?"

Levi opened the door and was further shocked to see Shane lying across his bed reading a book. A schoolbook! "Are you studying?" He knew it was a stupid question the second it tumbled from his mouth, but it had slipped out before he could stop it.

Shane gave him a look that told him he thought it was a pretty stupid question too. "No, I'm scuba diving, just don't tell the fish."

Levi had to bite the inside of his cheek to keep from smiling. He guessed he deserved that answer. "I brought you some stuff to put on your hands. It helps with the blisters." He tossed the tube onto the bed. "Tomorrow make sure you wear the gloves I gave you, okay?"

Shane glanced at the tube, but didn't touch it. "Whatever."

Levi looked around the room and frowned at the two suitcases still sitting on the floor. Shane hadn't unpacked. Nothing personal had been placed on top of the dresser or nightstand. The only things scattered about were a pile of schoolbooks and a bunch of CDs and cassettes. Shane obviously wasn't planning on staying long. "Want some company?"

"What time did you say we go to George's?"

"We start work at six-thirty." He cringed at Georgia's name being shortened to George, but didn't say anything. On the way home from work earlier he had given Shane a lecture on manners, common courtesy, and some basic work ethics. He only hoped tomorrow the boy would put some of that knowledge to good use.

Shane snapped the book closed. "Then I guess I'll go cruising dreamland."

Levi figured that was Shane's way of saying he was tired and in no mood for his company. What a surprise! "If you're going to bed, would you mind if I go out for a while?" Since he couldn't bridge any type of communication with Shane, maybe he could stop in at Georgia's and explain the situation better.

Shane shrugged. "Knock yourself out." He tossed the book onto the floor with the rest and pulled the light blanket up over his legs. "It's a free country."

Levi hid his disappointment. What had he been expecting, a plea not to leave? "I won't be gone long." He stepped back into the hallway. "I'll pick up some milk on the way home, okay?"

"Whatever." Shane gave a jaw-popping yawn, fluffed his pillow, and turned completely away from him.

So much for concern. "Good night then. I'll see you in the morning."

"Yeah."

Levi pulled into Georgia's driveway and asked himself for the third time what in the world he thought he was doing. It was nine-thirty at night and there was an excellent chance Georgia might not be home, or if she was, she might not be alone. He didn't want to know anything about her personal life. The less he knew, the better he might sleep.

Now that he was there, however, it didn't take the sharp mind of a Sherlock Holmes to figure out that Georgia was not only home, but also alone. Several lights in the house were lit, and only her car was parked in front of the garage. Now he could worry about interrupting her *doing* something personal, like showering. Sweat broke out across his brow as he visualized her standing under spraying water wearing nothing but a few stray soap bubbles and a welcoming smile. Oh hell, he really didn't want to think about her showering. His body could only withstand so much pressure, and he was already past his limit. He got out of the truck and approached the house.

Instead of walking around to the front, he stepped up onto the porch and headed for the French doors he had installed. They were open, with the screen door pulled shut and uncurtained. Light was pouring out of them onto the porch.

He stepped up to the doors, raised his hand to knock, and was rendered breathless.

Georgia was on the other side of the well-lit kitchen, standing on a chair and trying, with what appeared to be not too much success, to nail in a curtain rod bracket. The fact that she was trying her hand at simple carpentry didn't surprise him, it was the way her denim shorts were riding up the back of her thighs that caused the heated sensation roaring through his gut. As she stretched upward, her shirt rode up, too, leaving him an enticing view of a silky band of skin between the bottom of the shirt and the waistband of her shorts. Her blond hair was piled on top of her head in a helter-skelter fashion, and her curvy bottom wiggled provocatively, sending what blood remained in his head rushing to his groin.

Damn, the woman was a distraction even while hanging curtains! If she wasn't careful, she was going to lose her balance and end up with that cute little tush hitting the floor. Just the thought of her bruising that luscious seat had him knocking softly, so as not to startle her.

Nonetheless, Georgia nearly lost her balance as she quickly turned in the direction of the patio doors.

He didn't wait to be invited in; he opened the screen door and stepped into the kitchen. "Careful."

"Levi!" The bracket she had been trying to nail into place slipped and fell to the floor. A bent nail landed next to it. "What are you doing here? Did you forget something?"

He walked over to her and removed the hammer from her fingers, then bent to pick up the bracket. He had to chuckle as he also picked up three bent nails. Georgia might look like every man's fantasy, but she couldn't hammer worth a damn. Then again, most men wouldn't care if their fantasy woman could hammer in a nail. Levi figured he had to be lumped into the "most men" category. He straightened, avoiding looking at the provocative length of her legs, and glanced at the newly painted wall next to the window trim. Four little nail holes marked the surface. "I heard the wall screaming for me to save it."

"You empathize with your work? Must be the devil when you saw lumber in half." She glanced at the patio door. "Where's Shane?"

"Home sleeping." Without looking at her plump breasts, which were directly at his eye level, he helped her down from the chair. "I guess I pushed him a little more than he was accustomed to working." He stepped up onto the chair and positioned the bracket exactly where she had been trying to nail it.

"So tomorrow go easier on him."

"We'll see." He glanced at the lightweight curtain rod lying on the counter. "You aren't planning on hanging heavy curtains, are you? If you are, I should anchor the brackets in, not just nail them."

Georgia walked over to the kitchen table, where a mound of rods, brackets, and curtains were piled. She held up two small packages. "It's only a lace valance. I want as much natural light as possible in the room."

"Good." He reached for two nails from the small pile sitting on the window sill and proceeded to hang the bracket.

Georgia handed him the rod when he pointed to it. "You don't have to do this, Levi. I'm perfectly capable of hanging a few curtains."

He snapped the rod onto the brackets and studied the results. It appeared straight and even. "I know you are, but since I'm here, I might as well help you." He nodded to the other windows. "What goes on those two, the same thing?"

"Yes." She walked back to the table and picked up a matching rod and brackets as he carried the chair over to the next window. "Want to tell me why you're here?"

He ripped open the plastic bag that contained the brackets. "I want to apologize for forcing Shane on you this morning without any warning. I know his looks can be . . ." He rubbed the back of his neck, where there had been a knot of tension since his nephew had exited the plane. "Let's say, unsettling."

Georgia smiled. "Unsettling?"

His tension eased a bit with her smile. "What would you call it?"

"Expressing his individuality." She opened a

package containing a lace valance and eased it onto the rod.

"Really? I call it rebelling." He stepped up onto the chair and nailed the first bracket into place.

"As long as he's not hurting anyone by his appearance, I don't see anything wrong with it."

"You're not the one who had to go shopping with him the other night at the mall. You should have seen the looks he and I got from people in the stores."

"You? Why were people staring at you?"

"Half the adults glared at me as if I were some horrible parent for allowing my son to dress like that. The other half of the stares held nothing but sympathy."

Georgia chuckled. "Poor Levi. I'm not sure which would upset you more, the hostile ones or the sympathetic ones."

"Both." He moved the chair over a couple of feet and nailed in the other bracket. "But you're wrong about his appearance not hurting anyone. It is."

"Who, you? I didn't realize you had such thin skin."

Levi heard the disappointment in her voice, but he didn't defend himself against her comment. He really didn't care what other people thought about him or about Shane's appearance, but he had been shocked to see opinions expressed on just about everyone's faces wherever they went. "My skin's just fine. Shane's outrageous attire is hurting him. He was suspended from school because he refused to take off the mermaid earring."

"The school has something against mermaids?"

"No, the school has a policy against displaying bare-breasted women." He took the rod with the lace valance from her and snapped it onto the brackets. His fingers played with the valance until he thought it looked evenly gathered along the length of the rod.

"Oh, now I get it." She stood back and eyed the curtain. When Levi stepped down off the chair, she smiled at his handiwork. "Perfect." She reached for the little plastic bag containing the next set of brackets. "What happens when Shane's suspension is over?"

"They still won't allow him back into school until he takes off the mermaid earring."

"I gather he's still refusing."

Levi stepped back up onto the chair to nail in the next bracket. "I asked, pleaded, and offered to buy him another earring that wouldn't offend the school's dress code. He refused. Short of holding him down and yanking the well-endowed mythical creature from his ear, I don't know what else to do."

"What about his friends or girlfriend? Couldn't you have a talk with one of them and see if they could persuade Shane to take it off?"

"He doesn't have any friends. He just moved here two weeks ago from Iowa."

"I know it's none of my business and you can tell me so, but how did you end up being his guardian?" She started to gather another valance onto a rod.

Levi looked at her for a full minute before turning back to the bracket and pounding in a nail. "His parents, my sister Caroline and her husband Ben, were killed seven months ago while trying to rescue some livestock from their burning barn."

"Oh, Lord, Levi. I'm sorry."

He shrugged. He didn't know how to respond to her sorrow. A simple *thank you* seemed inappropriate. So what was a person to say? "Shane went to live with Ben's brother, his wife, and their three kids. The kids are about Shane's age and it meant he wouldn't have to transfer schools or leave his hometown. My parents and I thought it was the obvious solution and the best thing for Shane." He finished the first bracket and started to nail in the second. "About two months ago we were informed that Shane would be moving into Ben's parents' home. Again we thought it was the best thing for Shane and didn't question their decision. Two and a half weeks ago I received a phone call from Ben's parents begging me to take the boy. They told me Shane needed a firmer hand than what they could give since they're getting up there in age."

"You immediately said yes."

Levi glanced over his shoulder and saw her smile. At least she didn't look as if she were going to cry at any moment. He had noticed the tears that filled her eyes when he mentioned Shane's parents' deaths. Yes, he had immediately said yes. "Am I that obvious?"

"You might not understand Shane and his defiant attitude, but you love him. That much is obvious."

He finished nailing in the second bracket and reached for the rod she was holding. His gaze met and held hers. "Is it as obvious just how much I'm failing?"

Georgia shook her head. "You're not failing, Levi. Even the best of parents go through a rough patch."

"A rough patch?" He had to smile at that. "You think I'm going through a rough patch?" It didn't feel like a rough patch to him. It felt more like an out of control skid and he was heading for the back end of a gasoline truck. That damn red diamond placard with the flame was staring him straight in the face. He was just waiting for the explosion.

"From what I've seen of Shane," she said, "I would have to admit his appearance is . . . striking. But I also had a couple of opportunities to talk to him. He's polite, courteous, and seems to possess a sense of humor. I think underneath that spiked hair and dog collar is a fine young man."

Levi hung the rod on the brackets. "You should have seen him before the accident. He was on the honor roll, belonged to the 4-H, and had a dream of becoming a veterinarian. He passed tenth grade only because his grades had been so good at the beginning of the year, before the accident. Then he dropped out of the 4-H club and won't even look at an animal." Levi evened out the gathering of the valance and stepped down off the chair.

"All that sounds like a normal reaction to his parents' death, Levi." She busied herself with collecting the empty plastic bags and crunching them into a ball. "Did you consider family counseling?"

"Ben's brother and his wife tried it once. Shane was so obnoxious that they were too embarrassed to take him back."

"Sounds as if they're the ones who have the problem, not Shane."

Levi studied her in amazement for a full minute before it dawned on him. She was right! He wouldn't have been too embarrassed to keep bringing the boy back until they could work out some of Shane's problems. "You're right, Georgia." He had to wonder how she knew so much about kids. "How many brothers and sisters did you say you have?"

He had met her older brother once and didn't look forward to repeating that privilege. Morgan De Witt reminded him of a gangster from one of those old black-and-white movies. Brother and sister were complete opposites. Georgia was dainty, blond, and utterly graceful in her every move. Her brother topped Levi's own six-foot-one-inch frame by a good two inches, had nearly black hair and a rough-hewn face that gave Levi the impression Morgan had fought for everything he had ever wanted, and won.

"There's only Morgan and me," she answered.

Scratch the big extended family with lots of nieces and nephews. He'd known Morgan was single and extremely protective of his little sister. He just hadn't known how many "little sisters" there were. "You know a lot about troubled teens for not being around them much." He hadn't meant to unburden his soul on Georgia about Shane, but he was glad he had. He felt better for confiding in her. The problems weren't solved and no direction had been pointed out to him, but it didn't seem so hopeless any longer. Somehow, some way, he would get through to Shane.

Georgia lowered her gaze, but not before he saw the pain etched deep in her eyes. He had hurt her! But how? "Georgia?" He reached out a hand for her as she backed away.

She shook her head and hurried to the other side of the room. "Can I bribe you with a cup of coffee or a cold drink for hanging that last rod?" She glanced at the table where the rod lay.

He let her change the subject because he had

seen her pain. But one day soon he would find out what he had said to cause her grief. "Do you have any of the iced tea left over from this afternoon?"

Her smile was one of gratitude. "Coming right up."

He picked up the rod from the table and grinned at the printed instructions. It would take a scientist and a mathematician to figure them out. Unlike the others, this rod was an ornamental brass one that was to hold the curtains covering the patio doors. He glanced at the French doors, the rod, and the two packs of curtains still on the table and shook his head. What had he gotten himself into?

Ten minutes and eight totally inspired, but silent, curse words later, he nearly had the rod up. Georgia was driving him crazy. She buzzed around beneath him offering encouragement and tools he had absolutely no use for. He knew she was trying to help, but he didn't see it that way.

She was a distraction. Her perfume teased his senses and she was so encitingly close, he was amazed his knees hadn't buckled yet. With him standing on the chair, the top of her head came to his waist. He didn't want to think about what a provocative picture that created!

The temperature in the kitchen had to have risen twenty degrees in the last ten minutes. Perspiration clung to his brow, his hands were trembling, and every ounce of his will was ordering his body not to react to Georgia's nearness. Considering the view she had, he was going to embarrass himself in about two more minutes. His control was slipping, and slipping fast.

He tightened the last screw and quickly jumped down from the chair. "Why don't you put the curtains on the rod while I wash up?" He headed for the sink before she could respond. The fifteen-foot distance allowed him to breathe deeply without smelling her scent.

"They need to be ironed first." She reached for the two glasses of iced tea. "Thank you, Levi. I was afraid that last rod was going to give me some trouble, and I was right."

He dried his hands and took the glass she held out to him. "Thanks." He took a sip. "The rod wasn't that bad. I would have put it up for you tomorrow. All you had to do was ask." He didn't mind doing little things for Georgia that hadn't been included in the contract. She was forever offering him coffee and cold drinks. Out of all the people he had ever worked for, Georgia De Witt had to be one of the nicest. Her only competition came from Mrs. Lapp, who had been at least eighty-five and who had insisted on baking him chocolate chip cookies, his favorite, while he was in the middle of remodeling her kitchen. Mrs. Lapp still sent him a tin filled with her cookies every Christmas.

Georgia walked over to the table and pushed the curtains aside. "Do you want to sit?"

He wanted to do a lot of things with Georgia,

but sitting wasn't one of them. The room had become a little too warm for his comfort and his peace of mind. "How about if we take our drinks and go sit out on your porch?" he suggested, thinking there was a lot of truth in that old saying. *If you can't stand the heat, get out of the kitchen!*

SIX

Georgia relished the cool night air sweeping over her heated flesh, but it didn't help. Levi was too close. She could detect the faint scent of soap from his recent shower and maybe a hint of pine. Was it his aftershave? She didn't know. She had never smelled a man's cologne that reminded her of the forest without being overpowered by the scent and feeling as if she were buried under a pile of pine cones and peat. Levi smelled natural and clean. It was the most arousing fragrance. Great. She didn't need another one of her senses to become aroused whenever he was near.

She finished her glass of iced tea and carefully set it on the wooden porch, out of the swing's way. She would have preferred to stay inside the kitchen where it was well lit and the desire she felt for Levi could be semicontrolled. Temptation lurked in the dark. At least in her mind it did. She couldn't tell what Levi was thinking because she could barely see him, and he hadn't said more than two words since they sat down on the porch swing ten minutes ago.

She would love to know the real reason behind his visit. Shane's appearance, both at her house that morning and in Levi's life, had a lot to do with it. But was that all? Was Levi just looking for someone to talk to, someone to confide in, or was he there for another reason? Like the kiss they had shared the other day.

Please, she prayed, let it be the memory of the kiss that had brought him to her door this late in the evening! She wanted another one. Heck, she wanted a dozen more just like that one. Truth be told, she'd take a thousand, a million! She was a proud woman, but she wasn't above a little begging. Why else had he suggested they come outside if not to gaze at the moon and stars, start feeling romantic, and kiss?

Levi cleared his throat and placed his empty glass on the porch deck. His long legs pushed the swing into motion. "You really don't mind about Shane's working here for a few days, do you?"

So much for her dreams about hot kisses under the moon and stars. "Of course not. He seems like a good kid who's just a little confused. After everything he's been through this past year, it's completely understandable." At least she understood what Shane was going through. She had been down that lonely road herself.

"When you put it like that, you're right." Levi continued to rock the swing gently. "I guess I had envisioned picking up Shane from the airport and becoming an instant father. I pictured driving into Philadelphia or Baltimore to catch some major league baseball or football games. Maybe teaching him to drive a stick shift and helping him pick out his first car. You know, father things."

She felt Levi's helpless shrug shift the swing. "Have you found any common ground at all?"

"I don't even know where to start."

"You could start with asking him why he wants to be called 'Seaweed.' " That one had been driving her crazy, but she was too polite to ask the boy outright.

"What if he tells me he was a whale or something in a previous life?"

She couldn't help it. She burst out laughing at the whine in Levi's voice. The man had barely cringed when he whacked his thumb with a hammer the other week, and tonight he sat in the dark whining about missed baseball games and the strange workings of a sixteen-year-old's mind. "If that's his belief, my advice would be, don't argue about it with him." She chuckled again. "I would be curious about how he knew he had been a whale, or even what kind."

The toe of Levi's sneaker stopped the swing in midsway. "You have a beautiful laugh. You should gift it to the world more often."

The last little chuckle wrapped itself around

her tonsils and refused to emerge. He thought she had a beautiful laugh and she should gift it to the world more often? Oh my! What a wonderful way of phrasing it. If she wasn't already attracted to the darling man, she would be now. No one had ever complimented her laugh before. "Thank you."

"Why thank me? I only stated the truth." He sighed heavily and muttered, "Damn."

She could feel his gaze on her but couldn't make out his expression. The light pouring out of the French doors was too far away to do any good. "What's wrong?" His distress was almost tangible enough for her to touch it.

"I want to kiss you again."

Her heart climbed into her throat and she gripped her hands together to stop them from shaking. *Hallelujah!* Her strict proper upbringing went flying out of her head. "So who's stopping you?"

The swing shifted as Levi turned to face her. "I really shouldn't kiss you." She could see the silhouette of his hand as he ran it through his hair; she could hear the frustration in his voice. "I'm working for you."

"As of this moment you're fired." She moved a couple of inches closer. The soft denim of his jeans brushed against her bare thigh. "I'll rehire you in the morning. Be here by seven." It wasn't actual begging, but it was close.

Levi made a funny noise that sounded suspiciously like a laugh. "But I don't think . . . "

She laid a hand on his chest. "Good, don't think, Levi." She leaned in closer and smiled at the vibrations of his rapidly pounding heart beneath her palm.

"Oh, the hell with it." Levi hauled her into his arms and claimed her mouth.

As far as stating his intentions went, she had had more polished and sophisticated propositions, but none of them had affected her heart the way Levi's did. She felt the command of his kiss and willingly complied. Her arms slid around his neck as she opened her mouth and deepened the kiss. She wanted more. Dreamed of more. Meeting the thrust of his tongue, she demanded more.

Without breaking the kiss, Levi tightened his hold and pulled her sideways up onto his lap. The chains creaked noisily and the swing gave a couple of violent lurches before settling back down under their combined weight.

She snuggled against his chest and wildly ran her fingers through his soft short hair. Rock hard thighs cradled her bottom and her legs were stretched across the swing where she had been sitting moments before. She felt so small and feminine in Levi's embrace, yet so protected and safe.

He reached up and tugged at the elastic band holding her hair on the top of her head. The band released its hold and his fingers wove through her tousled hair. She playfully nipped at his lower lip and was rewarded with his groan. Lord, she had thought their kiss the other afternoon had been explosive. It was tame compared with what she was feeling now.

The sensitive peaks of her breasts were brushing against the solid wall of Levi's chest. The thin cotton blouse she had pulled on to combat the heat of the day now felt like a suit of armor. She wanted it removed, along with her bra and every other stitch of clothing she had on. She wanted Levi upstairs, in her bed, and in the same condition.

She wasn't a stranger to the physical aspects of love, but never before had she felt this burning need to satisfy the deep throbbing ache Levi's kisses aroused. An ache that was growing with intensity with every passing moment. Her hand cupped the back of his head and pulled him closer. She softly moaned his name.

He broke the kiss and skimmed a fiery string of moist nibbles down her throat to the valley between her breasts. Her shirt stopped his descent. His hand grasped the back of her thigh and slid upward. Roughened fingertips inched their way under the hem of her shorts.

She instinctively wiggled her bottom and was rewarded with Levi's groaning her name in near agony. Her mouth caressed his neck and her teeth toyed with his ear. She ran her tongue along the outer edge of his ear and felt the shudder that shook his body. It matched her own.

In the next instant strong hands grabbed her hips and lifted her from his lap. She landed gently on the swing as Levi leaped up and paced a couple yards away from her. The light behind him left him in shadows, so she couldn't see his face, but she could hear his breathing. It was labored and harsh. Why had he stopped? "Levi?"

He turned to face the open yard, away from her. It was as if he couldn't stand the sight of her. "I've got to go."

Her hands clenched into fists and she willed herself not to scream. He couldn't be serious and just walk away, could he? "Where?"

"Home." He continued to look in the direction of the barn. "Shane's in the house, and I really don't like to leave him alone for too long."

She knew it was a lie. Levi might not want to leave Shane alone for too long, but that wasn't the reason he was leaving. "Don't hide behind the boy, Levi. He wouldn't appreciate being used like that." She pulled up her legs and wrapped her arms around her knees. So much for feeling safe and protected in his embrace. She now felt opened and exposed. Levi knew how much she wanted him, yet he wanted to go home.

He turned in her direction. "Dammit, Georgia!" he fairly shouted. "That shouldn't have happened!"

She raised her chin and shouted right back,

"Dammit, Levi, it did." She wasn't going to be nice and act the part of the *lady*, and allow Levi to climb back into his pickup and head home. She wasn't going to let him off the hook that easy. He had been the one to start it by coming over, luring her out into the dark, and then tempting her with mind-numbing kisses that promised paradise. She wanted to taste that paradise.

He jammed his hands into his jeans pocket and stared at her for a long time before turning away once again. "You're right, Georgia. It did happen."

Her gut was telling her he was about to continue in a direction she would rather he didn't. "Don't you dare apologize for kissing me again, Levi. You kissed me, and I kissed you back. We both know there was mutual pleasure in the experience." She rested her chin on her drawn-up knees and asked, "So what are you going to do about it?" She already knew what she wanted to do about it. Her solution contained a lot less clothes and a set of satin sheets.

"I'm not going to do anything about it."

"You're going to pretend it never happened?"

"No, that would be impossible and we both know it." He rocked back on his heels. "I have my hands full with converting your barn into one of the county's leading antique shops. My life has been turned upside down with Shane's arrival, not that I'm complaining. There just isn't any time left over for anything or anyone else, Georgia. I'm sorry."

"Not half as sorry as I am." He was making excuses. Work, Shane, and time. They were all excuses. Excuses to keep her out of his life. She didn't need him to hit her over the head with a brick. She knew when she wasn't wanted. "It's getting late, Levi. I'll see you and Shane in the morning." It wasn't late. It was barely ten o'clock.

"I . . . " He shook his head, as if to clear it. "All right, Georgia. We'll be here bright and early." He stepped off the porch. "Make sure you lock up good."

"I already have one brother. I'm not looking for another." She stayed on the swing and watched as he walked to his truck. As he opened the driver door, she softly called, "Good night."

In the faint glow from the overhead cab light his face appeared all sharp edges and angles. Shadows slashed across his face, giving it a dark and dangerous appearance. His voice was low and harsh as it rode the night breeze. "Sleep tight."

Within a moment, he was gone. She sat on the swing as he backed out of the driveway and watched as his taillights disappeared around the bend in the road. She had to wonder what it was about her that drove good, decent men away. Men with ulterior motives gravitated toward her, lured by the scent of the De Witt fortune and her vulnerable heart. But the nice ones always left, leaving her frustrated and strangely unsatisfied.

What in the hell was wrong with her that men like Adam, her ex-fiancé, and now Levi left without ever making love to her?

Levi stood in the shadows of the barn's doorway and listened to Georgia and Shane as they shared a snack in the shade of a towering maple tree. Had it only been two days since he had shared sizzling kisses with Georgia on her porch swing under the stars? It felt like hours ago. His mouth could still taste her. His body could still feel her.

The daylight hours spent working at her place, with her so near, were bad, but they were nothing compared with the nights he spent alone in his bed staring at the ceiling and thinking of her, dreaming of her. The temperature that afternoon was pushing the high eighties, but it had nothing on the heat he was feeling just looking at her.

He watched fascinated as she laughed at something Shane said. He was too far away to hear their conversation, but he could tell Georgia was enjoying herself, and his nephew seemed totally captivated by her. In the weeks since Shane had moved in with him, never once had the boy displayed one ounce of humor. Judging from Georgia's laugh, someone would think the boy was a born comedian.

Levi didn't want to think about her laugh or

the way her face lit up when she smiled. He especially didn't want to think about the way his gut clenched with the desire to hear that laugh again and again. It was a dangerous craving for a man determined to remain uninvolved with any woman. But then again, Georgia had gotten under his skin faster than any other woman alive, and that included his ex-wife. The amazing part was she and Shane were hitting it off remarkably well.

They should have looked ridiculous sitting under the tree enjoying the shade and a cool drink. Georgia had been out all morning and was still dressed in one of those flowing silk skirts that ended at midcalf and boasted a gardener's delight of multicolored flowers. Her blouse was emerald green and it shimmered under the bright glare of the sun. Gold bracelets glimmered on her wrist. She looked incredibly beautiful and innocent.

Shane looked as if he belonged on one of those TV music channels, shouting lyrics that had censors going ballistic and politicians screaming about the moral decline of the nation. His jeans were so baggy another person could have climbed in there with him, and there would still be room left over. He had ripped the sleeves off his black T-shirt and was covered in dust and debris from working. His hair was still spiked, due to half a bottle of mega-hold gel, and half a dozen earrings, including the bare-breasted mermaid, still dangled from his ear. He looked ridiculous sitting beside Georgia, but he didn't seem to notice. Neither did she.

The only one having a problem with their budding friendship was Levi. Apparently he was the only one who saw the three of them for what they were; the socialite, the hired help, and the smart-mouthed punk.

He stepped out of the shadows and closer to the mismatched pair. He was curious about what they were talking about. Shane never talked to him at home or even at work. His nephew considered grunting to be a verbal communication skill.

Georgia saw Levi leave the barn and walk closer to her and Shane. She tried to ignore the leap her heart took and concentrated on what the boy was saying about some rodent's bones he had discovered while working on the barn.

"So I can keep the bones?" Shane asked.

"By all means. You may keep any bones you find." She shuddered at the thought of having animal bones in her new shop. "In fact, Seaweed, I insist you remove *all the bones* from the barn."

Shane grinned. "Cool." He leaned back on his elbows and studied the leaves over his head.

She noticed that Levi was hovering in the background, close enough to listen, but not close enough to participate. For the past two days she had been going slowly out of her mind, thanks to Levi. The more she thought about him, the angrier she became. Who did he think he was, kissing her senseless, then just leaving her like that?

Any idiot could see he had been avoiding her for the past two days, which was fine by her. The more Levi avoided her the more Shane sought out her company.

Her gaze settled on the boy, correction, young man. Shane Weaver was definitely in the young man category. His past held pain, which no one would deny, but his future held promise. She hadn't known Shane's parents, but she would wager one of her shops that they had loved him totally and that the feeling had been mutual. Shane wouldn't be rebelling the way he was if he hadn't loved them very much. His parents probably had dreamed about his future and what he would make of his life. In his own way Levi was carrying on in his sister's absence. Levi cared what happened to Shane, or he wouldn't be banging heads with the boy. The start to a bright future was a solid foundation, which included a good education. Shane couldn't get an education, good or otherwise, as long as he was suspended, and he was going to stay suspended until he removed the mermaid earring.

"Seaweed, can I ask you a personal question?" So far all their conversations had revolved around mundane everyday things, and she had religiously called him by his preferred name, Seaweed. Levi stubbornly still called him Shane and the boy just as stubbornly refused to answer. Her addressing him as Seaweed might be the reason he actually talked to her.

He turned his head and studied her for a moment. "Shoot."

"What's your girlfriend think about your choice in earrings?" She couldn't imagine any young woman liking the busty mermaid.

"Don't have a girlfriend." He picked up a small pebble and rolled it between his fingers while studying the distant hills. "Don't even know any kids from this stupid hick town." The pebble went sailing through the air.

She ignored the comment about Reinholds' being a hick town. From what Levi had told her, the town in Iowa where Shane was from was even smaller and more rural. "I'm sure you're going to be making lots of friends in school." She could have pointed out that he would have to be in school to meet them, but held that thought. Shane was intelligent enough to figure that one out for himself. "I was just curious about what girls think about your earrings, that's all."

Shane's chin rose and he glared at her. "You don't like my earrings?"

"Quite the opposite. Lots of men are wearing earrings nowadays and many women find them attractive. I especially like the silver hoop and the amber stud."

"You do?"

"Sure, why would I lie about it?" She nodded toward his left ear, where the mermaid dangled. "I was mainly curious about how girls react to the mermaid earring."

He touched the tail of the mermaid. "You don't like mermaids?"

"I do. I happen to appreciate legends and myths. I have a Pegasus lapel pin forged out of the finest silver. A silversmith in Lancaster custom designed it for me." She knew Levi was listening to their every word. She also knew that Shane hadn't spotted him yet, so there was a chance he would continue to talk.

Shane frowned at her. "Why would girls react any different toward the mermaid than any other of my earrings? Earrings are earrings."

"Some girls might object to the . . . let's say *charms* of the watery maiden." She knew Shane understood exactly what she was referring to by the tide of red sweeping up his face. "Some girls might actually think that was how you viewed all women."

"As mermaids?" Shane looked confused.

"No, as sex objects." She refused to look in Levi's direction. She knew she was stepping on some very sensitive ground, but Shane's suspension was up in two days and she wanted to see the boy back in school studying and making friends. "When I was your age my older brother, Morgan, had to meet all the boys I went out with or I wasn't allowed out."

"Boy, that sucks. I bet you hated him."

"No, I knew he loved me enough to care. The sad part is that parents, and even protective older brothers, don't have a whole lot to judge a kid on besides appearances, the way they talk, and what kind of car they're driving. It's kind of like judging a book by its cover. A person could miss some great reads that way." Levi had told her how intelligent Shane was. She prayed he would pick up on her subtle hints about his appearance because she really didn't want to come right out and tell the boy that if he had shown up on her doorstep when she was sixteen, Morgan would have thrown him off the property and none too gently.

"What about your dad? Didn't he care who you went out with?"

Pain lashed at her heart. Pain from the past, pain of the present for things that could never be, and the pain she was going to cause Shane by opening up his recent wound. "My parents were both killed when I was sixteen. Morgan raised me after that."

Shane's brown eyes darkened with fresh hurt. His voice cracked with emotion as he softly asked, "How did they die?"

"Car accident." She held Shane's gaze, but she knew Levi had quietly made his way to the tree to join them. "We were driving back from Princeton University. Morgan had graduated that afternoon. My parents' backseat was loaded with Morgan's clothes and stuff. I got to ride with Morgan in his little sports car. We left the campus about five minutes after them. Outside Philadelphia we got tied up in a traffic jam for an hour. We watched the ambulances come and go and we didn't even know it was them until the wrecker went by towing their car. By then it was too late. My mother was gone and Dad died later that night in the hospital."

Tears filled Shane's eyes. Big fat tears that threatened to spill over at any moment. He didn't seem to notice, just kept studying her face. "Do you still miss them?"

His painful loss was evident and it appeared too heavy for his young shoulders to carry. She wanted to relieve him of some of his burden, but knew she couldn't. Only he could lessen the weight by sharing it. "I miss them every day, Shane. The pain isn't so bad as it was when I first lost them, but I still miss them." She watched as his hand trembled slightly and willed herself not to reach out to him. He would have to make the first move. "At first I was so afraid, but I had my brother to hold my world together for me." She held her hand out and silently willed Shane to grab it. "I can't imagine what you must be going through."

Shane glared at her hand and then at his uncle, who had knelt beside her. "Great, group sympathy!" He jumped to his feet and swiped his knuckles across his eyes. "You're right, George, you can't imagine what I've been going through. You had your brother while I have no one." He snarled at his uncle. "I won't even give you another week before you ship me off to another unsuspecting relative."

Georgia glanced at Levi. He looked shocked at the viciousness of his nephew's attack. "That's not fair, Shane. Levi isn't going to be shipping you off to anywhere."

"Yes he will. Just like my other uncle and his wife and their three precious children. Just like my grandparents who cried all the way to the airport professing their love while shoving me on a plane to fly me out of their lives." Shane turned away and stormed back into the barn.

Georgia grabbed Levi's arm to stop him from rising and following his nephew. "Give him a while to calm down before going after him, Levi. He's a proud boy and he doesn't want you to see him cry."

Levi stared at her incredulously. "He can't really believe I'm going to send him off to someone else, can he?"

"I'm afraid so. It's what he's learned. As soon as there's trouble or he doesn't fit into someone's neat and orderly idea of what he should be, he's been packed up and shipped off." She could tell that idea didn't sit too well with Levi. "It also could explain why he's so rebellious and has managed to get himself suspended the first week of school."

"He expects me to send him away, doesn't he?"

"To his way of thinking, the sooner the better. Why make friends here when he's not planning on sticking around?"

Levi jammed his fingers through his hair and muttered a string of foreign words. By his tone, she would guess they wouldn't be said over the Thanksgiving Day turkey. She raised an eyebrow. "German?"

"Pennsylvania Dutch. My grandfather had a colorful vocabulary." He stared at the barn. "I have to go talk to him."

"I know." Shane wasn't going to appreciate his uncle following him into the barn. Later on he would, but not right now.

Levi slowly turned and faced her. His hand cupped her cheek. "I'm sorry Shane's loss has re-opened your pain." His thumb brushed her cheekbone. "I can see the sadness in your eyes."

Darn it! If he didn't stop it, she was going to start blubbering like a fool. "Wounds need to be opened every once in a while, Levi. If they aren't exposed to fresh air they tend to fester and grow." She reached up and lowered his hand. It felt warm and strong, and any other time she would have clung to it. "Go talk with Shane. He needs you now, more than ever." She released his hand.

"Will you be all right?"

"I'm a big girl, Levi." She turned away from the tender look on his face. "I'll be fine."

She studied the distant hills covered with trees as Levi stood and headed after Shane. Within the next two months the rich green foliage would be gone and the hillsides would be ablaze with the colors of autumn. She was looking forward to the crisp autumn days and the spectacular view. Maybe with the cool nights she would sleep better.

Sighing wearily, she pushed herself up, then brushed off her skirt and reached for the empty glasses. Break time was over and she had a mountain of paperwork to tackle before heading to Kentucky the next morning for an array of estate sales.

SEVEN

Georgia opened the screen door and stepped out onto the porch, carefully balancing a mug of coffee. She glanced up at the sun riding high in the sky. She had slept the morning away. Considering she had driven through the night to get home, she hadn't been too surprised when she rolled over in bed and saw the red illuminating numbers on her clock reading eleven-thirty. When she had finally crawled into bed, the sky hadn't been lighting up, but dawn had been just around the corner. The twelve-hour drive home from Kentucky had been worth it, though, just to sleep in her own bed.

The constant buying trips were becoming more of a burden than an adventure. She used to look forward to the different estate sales and auctions, the thrill of discovering and bidding on unique items for her stores. Now she only looked forward to heading home, sleeping in her own bed, and seeing Levi. Maybe it was time to let Francine get her wish and go on a buying trip.

Darn Levi and his ability to make her think about him even when she was four states away.

She looked over at the barn and noticed some of the changes that had taken place since she'd been gone. In the past three days numerous boards had been replaced on the outside of the barn, and a couple of holes had been cut into one side for windows. Levi and she had both agreed that the place needed windows, lots of windows. She wanted natural light to flood the inside from all four main walls and from skylights. A series of six skylights were planned for the back slope of the roof.

Levi's truck was parked in front of the barn, where a small asphalt parking lot would be going. She could hear the muffled pounding of a hammer. Only one hammer. Which meant Shane had removed the earring and was back in school, or he was working on something that didn't make noise. She hoped that he and Levi had come to some type of understanding and that the boy was back in school making friends.

She wanted to go check on the progress of her shop and to see if Shane was indeed in school, but she headed for the porch swing instead. Both of those reasons would only be excuses to see Levi. She needed time to analyze this deep-seated need to see the man who claimed he was never going to kiss her again. Why hadn't she ever realized before that she had masochistic tendencies?

The chains on the swing creaked as she finished her coffee and watched the barn, speculating what might have transpired between Levi and his nephew during her absence. It really wasn't any of her business, and she would be the first to admit it, but it didn't stop her from caring. Both for Shane and for Levi.

Shane had a bond with her. At a very vulnerable time of their lives, they had both lost their parents in tragic accidents. She, luckily, had had her brother to help her. Shane had Levi. She only hoped the boy realized Levi was on his side and wouldn't alienate his uncle completely.

Levi, on the other hand, totally confused her. The man appeared to be a loner, yet he opened his home unquestioningly to his nephew. There was a sense of responsibility, of duty there, but it went further than that. It came from his heart. Deep inside, Levi was a family man, even if it was an unconventional family. The astonishing part was, while she had been traveling through Kentucky and attending sales and auctions, she learned something very important about herself. For the first time in her life, she wanted a family of her own. She wanted Levi and Shane.

A family! If that concept didn't throw her for a loop, nothing would. She had always pictured her future holding a husband and maybe a dog or a cat. But kids! No way. She'd never had the burning desire to get pregnant, go through hours of agony, and then lose night after night of sleep just to hold up a crying infant to the world and say, see, I did this. Millions of women every year had babies, but not many of them could build an antique business from the ground up. She could, and she was darn proud of that fact. So why now, on the dawning of her crowning jewel of a shop, her greatest dream, was she feeling so unfulfilled?

She frowned at the mug still clutched in her hands. Baffled, she watched as two lone drops of coffee rolled across the white ceramic bottom as she tilted the mug. They converged and made one large drop. A single unit made out of individual drops. Just like a family. Boy, she was really losing it if she could analyze the family structure by the cold coffee rolling around in her mug.

"Just get up?"

She snapped her head around and saw Levi. He was standing at the foot of the porch steps, watching her study her cup. She glared down at the mug and noticed the drop still held together, even after her violent jerk. "A couple minutes ago," she answered. Covering a yawn, she placed the empty mug on the floor. "How's everything going here?" Levi looked tired, hot, and incredibly kissable. She wanted to jump up from the swing, wrap her arms around his neck, and welcome herself home with the taste of his mouth.

"Good." He stepped up onto the porch, removed his tool belt, and sat down next to her.

"The company that is going to install the skylights and repair the slate shingles on the roof was here yesterday. They said it will be sometime next week before the work can begin."

She refused to read anything into the fact that he'd sat down next to her. There wasn't anywhere else for him to sit besides the floor. "That fit in with your schedule?"

"Sure, I'm flexible."

She shot a quick glance at his thighs and remembered their strength. He was about as flexible as the rock of Gibraltar, but she kept that opinion to herself. She turned her attention to the barn. "Shane back to school?"

"He went back yesterday."

"I gather he took off the earring."

"He took out four of them the day you left."

"Congratulations. Whatever you said to him must have worked."

"It wasn't me, it was you." Levi gazed at her for a long moment. "I never would have thought of telling him that girls might not appreciate the mermaid's nudity. I was more worried about the school board's opinion."

"Oh." She gave a small shrug. "I was just relaying the female point of view, that's all."

"Hmmm . . . " Levi leaned back and stared up at the painted ceiling of the porch while using his legs to keep the swing going. "I found out why he wants to be called Seaweed."

"Why?" Levi was acting awfully strange. He

was talking about Shane, yet he didn't seem to want to be. He had the look of a man with something entirely different on his mind.

"It was a nickname his father gave him about four months before the accident. Shane had just gotten a horse named Great White, because of its color. About a week after they got him, Shane wasn't careful and Great White nipped at his hand. His father teased him and said he must have smelled like seaweed. Shane teased his father right back and informed him that great white sharks are carnivores, not herbivores. As a playful retaliation for the lecture, his father started calling him Seaweed."

Georgia could feel the tears forming in the backs of her eyes and willed them not to fall. Her own father used to call her Pumpkin when she was little, and he occasionally slipped with the nickname after she entered her teens. She would give up everything she owned just to hear him call her that one more time while being pulled into his arms. Or to smell again the sweet lilac fragrance her mother adored. Every spring when the lilacs were in bloom she ached for her mother.

She understood Shane's need to keep a part of his father's memory alive. "Was Great White one of the animals his parents were trying to save?"

"Yes, along with about a dozen or so other strays and wounded animals. It's my understanding that Shane had quite a collection of animals in the barn when it went up."

"That explains both the defiant and the indifferent attitude."

"What does?" Levi gave her a confused look. "Shane's rebelling against society because he lost his horse and a dozen or so other animals he was nursing back to health?"

"No." She stared at Levi and realized he hadn't a clue. No one had a clue! Not Shane's grandparents, or his uncle and aunt who had dragged him to a psychologist and then were too embarrassed to return. Lord, was the entire family so thick-headed they couldn't see what was sitting directly in front of them?

Or maybe she saw because she knew what Shane must be going through. Guilt was a terrible burden to carry around, especially on shoulders as young as Shane's.

"Care to explain yourself?" Levi asked as he stopped the swing with the toe of his work boot.

"Shane feels guilty."

"About what?"

"One of two things, or possibly both. He either feels guilty for his parents' death or he feels guilty for not being there and perishing with them."

"That's insane! Why would he feel guilty about their deaths or not dying with them?"

"No, it's not insane, Levi. It's how the mind works, especially a young mind." She bit her lower lip for a moment, then told him her darkest secret. A secret so terrible that it had taken a top adolescent psychologist two years to pull it from her, and then, in the ultimate act of love for a brother who had stood beside her during those turbulent years, she had confessed it to Morgan. He had understood. She didn't know if Levi would, but for Shane's sake she had to try. The pain couldn't hurt her any longer.

"You heard me tell Shane about how my parents were killed when I was sixteen?" She didn't wait for his response, she knew he had. "I didn't turn rebellious like Shane. I did the opposite. I became invisible." She saw Levi's astonished look and clarified. "Not literally invisible, but figuratively. I stopped going to school. No matter what Morgan tried, it didn't work. There wasn't any form of punishment greater than what I was punishing myself with. Eventually Morgan had to have me tutored at home, and even then it still didn't go smoothly.

"I didn't talk for weeks at a time. The more Morgan pulled me close, the more I ignored him as if he weren't there. As if I weren't there. I felt I didn't deserve his love, or anyone else's love."

Levi captured her chin in the palm of his hand and forced her to look straight at him. "Why?"

"Because I felt guilty for my parents' death and the fact that I wasn't killed with them."

"You wanted to die with them?"

"At the time, yes." She blinked back the tears that were pooling in her eyes. "You see, I should have been in the car with them. I rode up to the

college with them and I should have been there
for the return trip. Only I weaseled a ride with my
brother in his brand-new graduation present. I
was envious of his car because I had just gotten
my license but wasn't allowed to have a car of my
own. They said I had to wait until my eighteenth
birthday. We left five minutes behind our parents
because I was arguing with Morgan and trying to
convince him to let me drive. He wouldn't."

"Your brother made the right decision. You
told Shane his car was some red-hot sports car."

She gave him a fleeting smile. "It was. Anyway, when we came upon the traffic jam, Morgan
and I still weren't talking. It wasn't until we saw
our parents' car being towed that we realized they
were involved. I sat there frozen while Morgan
grabbed the first police officer he could find and
demanded to know where our parents were.
Twenty minutes later we arrived at the hospital.
Our mother had already died on the way to the
hospital, and Dad passed away that night."

"You didn't cause the accident, Georgia.
There shouldn't have been any guilt."

"I know that now, but back then I came up
with hundreds of reasons why I was at fault. I
should have argued with my father to drive *his*
car, and then he wouldn't have been in that precise spot at that precise instant to be in that accident. I should have been in the car with them and
maybe I could have seen and warned them about
the drunk who was about to run the red light. Any

way I looked at it, it was always my fault. I should have prevented it and if I couldn't have prevented it, I should have died with them."

Levi's thumb stroked her bottom lip where her teeth had worried a small indentation. "I'm sorry about your parents, Georgia. But I'm awfully glad you weren't in the car with them."

She sniffled. "You sound like Morgan. Back then I hated myself, and I hated Morgan for dragging me to every doctor or person he thought could help me combat my grief. Back then I didn't want Morgan's love. I was scared to love him for fear something terrible would happen to him and then I would truly be alone in the world. I was scared he would figure out that there were a dozen things I could have done that day to save our parents' lives and he would hate me as much as I hated myself. The harder I pushed him away, though, the harder he pulled me close."

"Remind me to thank your brother one day."

"He'd probably pass out knowing that I'd confided all my old fears to you." Morgan De Witt would never pass out, but he would be shocked by her confession. Morgan had been a pillar of strength throughout those terrible years. Never once had he given up on her. There wasn't a person alive who could bring him to his knees. "I only told you about my parents' deaths so you could understand Shane better. See that he gets the help he needs to handle his grief."

"You think he feels guilty for not being there to help his parents fight the fire?"

"Count on it. He probably feels more guilt than I ever felt because they were *his* animals his parents were trying to save. Imagine the hundreds of things he's feeling he should have done differently."

"Lord," Levi looked shaken. "Why didn't I see it sooner?"

"Every child reacts differently to grief. Some let the tears flow and heal slowly. Others, like myself, turn inward, afraid the world would see our guilt. And some are like Shane, who turn outward and push everyone away from them by their rebellious acts and indifferent attitude."

"So what you're saying is Shane is pushing me away because . . . "

"Because he's afraid to care about you. He's afraid he'll lose you too. He doesn't feel worthy of your or anyone else's love. Not even an animal's. You said he had a dozen stray and wounded animals before the fire, and now he won't even look at one. I'm not an expert on this, but it seems reasonable to assume he probably feels he let the animals down too."

"So what's your advice? Psychological help?"

"Definitely, plus a healthy dose of love. Don't let him push you away, Levi. If he's the family you want, you're going to have to fight for him. His uncle and grandparents shipping him off to other

relatives only proved his point that he is un-
wanted and unloved."

"Christmas. Now I have to make up for their
mistakes."

"Don't blame them, Levi. They didn't know
what they were doing." In her experience, blame
never solved anything.

Levi sighed and stared off into the distance. "I
know. His grandparents and aunt and uncle do
love him. They called him the other day to see
how he's making out in school. Amazingly, Shane
actually said more than a dozen words to them."

"See?" She grinned. "It's going to work out
all right."

"Oh, yeah?" Levi brushed back a wisp of her
hair that the breeze blew across her cheek. "He
told them how I've been busting his ass working
all day and then making him study all night."

"Oops, maybe you should ease up a little on
him."

It was Levi's turn to grin. "Naw. The boy actually had pride in his voice when he told them.
Of course, he would never admit it, but I have the
feeling he likes the hard manual work. It releases
a lot of pent-up frustrations in a person when you
tear down a wall."

"Sounds like you're talking from experience."

"Yes, ma'am." His grin slowly faded. "I've
been knocking down more than a few walls of my
own these past weeks."

Her snappy response was stopped in her

throat by the heat burning in his eyes. Whatever Levi's frustrations were, they were solely directed at her. She had no idea if that was good or bad. Since she couldn't think of one frustration that was good, she had to assume he wasn't happy about them. By the look on his face she couldn't tell if he wanted to kiss her or strangle her.

She wasn't sure if she was strong enough to fall into the vortex of his kisses only to be brushed aside again. She wanted the kisses. She wanted more than kisses, much more. But for some reason Levi didn't. Oh, he physically wanted them, there was no way for him to hide his response to her. They struck sparks off each other better than a match on a striker board. Mentally, though, was another story. Something was holding him back, and it wasn't all because she happened to be his current boss.

She glanced at his tempting lips, remembering the taste of him, and willed herself to be strong. Her gaze flew upward to encounter his hungry look as she blurted out the first thing that came to her mind. "Do you want something cold to drink?"

Levi looked as if he were ready to explode, but he pushed himself off the swing and said, "Sure."

She hurried into the kitchen and opened the refrigerator door. She could feel him standing directly behind her. "What would you like? I have soda, iced tea, or milk."

"None of the above."

She glanced over her shoulder and was startled to see how close he was standing to her. Not even an inch separated them. She straightened up, but he didn't step back. "None?"

He gently pushed the white refrigerator door closed. "What I want isn't in there, Georgia."

"What is it that you want?" She stepped away from him and felt the cool door against her back. She had to look up to meet his gaze. His face was temptingly close, but not as close as it had been in her dreams. His jaw was tight with determination and his lower lip was seductively full. Golden strands wove their way through his neatly trimmed chestnut hair. A slight wave fell across his forehead, begging for her touch.

"You," he answered.

Heat from his body engulfed her like a tidal wave. Hope rushed up to meet the heat. "Me?"

"It's the wrong time, Georgia, and the last thing I want is to get involved with you."

So much for secret fantasies. "Gee, Levi, you say the sweetest things."

"I don't know any flowery words or pretty speeches. Everything I say probably comes out all wrong, and I'm sorry for that. But the one thing you can count on from me is the truth."

"So, what you're trying to tell me, in your unpoetic way, is that it's the wrong time in your life, and you don't want to become involved with me?" She could handle that if that was the way he felt. So why was she practically pinned to the refrigerator door by his body? His very aroused, masculine, and incredibly tempting body.

"Yes and no." He placed both hands on the door, one on either side of her head, and captured her gaze with his.

She nervously licked her lips. His mouth was less than six inches away from hers. "Your truth is confusing me, Levi."

"I know, and I'm sorry." His thigh brushed against hers. "This is definitely the wrong time in my life, Georgia."

"Because of Shane?" Her knees trembled and she arched her hips away from the door.

"Partly, but I would love to have known you sixteen years ago."

"I wasn't any fun sixteen years ago." She had to wonder what had happened sixteen years ago to make him feel that had been the right time to know her.

"Are you any fun now?" His fingertips caressed her cheek and the side of her neck.

Lord, how she wanted to have some fun with Levi. "That depends."

"On what?"

"Why you don't want to get involved with me?" Was there something so drastically wrong with her that Levi wouldn't cross the line of friendship?

"I can't give you what you want, Georgia."

"What is it that you think I want?" She wanted a lot of things from Levi, the first one being a night, a week, oh hell, a year in bed relieving the frustration he had managed to build inside her.

"I can't give you a commitment." His thumb slowly and seductively rubbed against her neck.

She hadn't been expecting a declaration of love and a marriage proposal on bended knee. "I don't remember asking for one." The warmth from his thumb was driving her crazy. So much heat from just a little movement. Would she feel that heat everywhere he touched?

"You're the kind of woman who deserves more than I could give."

At first she thought he was referring to financial security, but then it dawned on her that he wasn't the type of man easily impressed or swayed by the almighty dollar. Levi made his own way in the world, and was proud of that fact. He wouldn't consider her bank account as an asset. In fact, it was probably more of a liability as far as he was concerned.

"What exactly are you willing to give?" She lightly pressed her hips against his, to emphasize the question, and smiled at his sudden intake of breath. Denim brushed denim. Where he was rock hard, she was invitingly soft. She hadn't a lot of experience seducing a man, but then, she'd never wanted a man as much as she wanted Levi.

His gaze turned intense. She could feel the tight grip he had on his control and she wanted to shatter it. His hips nudged against hers and she was left in no doubt of his arousal. She gave in to temptation and pushed the silky lock of hair back off his forehead.

"I could give you satisfaction." His voice sounded as if it came from a bottomless well; deep, dark, and incredibly dangerous.

She didn't doubt that for a moment. She wanted more from him than a satisfying romp upstairs, but she was willing to begin there. "If that's what you want to give . . . " she wrapped her arms around his neck and pulled his head down closer, "then you won't get any arguments from me."

He chuckled and brushed his lips over hers. "I've been working in a barn for five hours straight." His hands gripped her hips and held them still. "I need a shower and change of clothes."

"I've got a shower upstairs." She playfully nipped at his lower lip. "Hell, I've even got a whirlpool tub that gives a new meaning to 'scrubbing bubbles.' "

This time Levi returned her frisky teasing with a playful nip of his own. "I know. I've been fantasizing about your being in that tub for the past month."

She stretched up on her toes and tried to recapture his mouth. "Naughty boy." When he wouldn't cooperate she skimmed a finger down the front of his blue chambray shirt and toyed with each button on her way to his belt buckle.

What she knew about the seduction game came from the movies and television. So she pouted sexy, or what she hoped was sexy and not as if she had an abscessed tooth, batted her eyelashes and purred, "If you ask real nicely, I might even scrub your back."

He took a giant step back and came up against the cooking island he had installed a week earlier. "We can't . . . you know . . . now!"

"Why not?" Geez, she offered to scrub the man's back and practically climbed into his shirt and he said not now. Next he'd be complaining about a headache.

He ran his fingers through his hair and took a deep breath. "Because I'm supposed to be working."

"I'll dock your pay."

He glared at her. "Shane's coming directly here after school. He's working for me a couple of hours every day and on Saturdays because he wants to save up and buy a car."

She glanced at the clock. "That's four hours from now."

"Hell, Georgia, I don't have anything! Do you?"

She was momentarily thrown off balance by that one. *He didn't have anything on him!* She could feel the fiery flush sweeping up her cheeks as she realized what he meant. Levi wasn't the type of man who carried around protection in his back pocket, just in case he got lucky. The way today was going, he would have been lucky in five minutes. "I don't have anything either." This might be the nineties, but she'd rather have all her hair fall out before she would walk into the local Uni Mart and buy a pack of condoms.

"That's settled then." Levi headed for the patio doors, but then stopped in the middle of the room, marched back to her, and hauled her into his arms. The kiss he planted on her surprised mouth singed the lace edging of her panties before he released her with great reluctance. "I might never have been a Boy Scout, Georgia, but I promise you the next time you offer to scrub my back, I won't be unprepared."

She touched her mouth with the tip of her fingers and grinned as he walked out the door.

Georgia heard the noisy air brakes of the school bus as it pulled up in front of her house. She rose from the kneeling position she had been in for the past ten minutes and brushed off her hands. A neat pile of weeds lay at her feet and her colorful rows of impatiens and petunias looked as if they could breathe again. She smiled as Shane vaulted out of the bus and into her yard. He walked directly to her.

"Hi, George. It sure gets lonely around here when you're away."

"Hello to you too, Shane. I see they let anyone back into that school." Smiling, she nodded at his ear where only a small silver stud and a miniature skull remained. If she wasn't mistaken his spiked Mohawk wasn't quite as high as before, either, and there was only one dog collar wrapped around his neck. She noticed Levi had left the barn and was making his way toward them. "You had your uncle to keep you company."

Shane actually smiled at Levi. "He's been a grouch the entire time you were gone."

She raised one eyebrow and grinned at Levi, who had joined them and had heard Shane's comment. "Really? How can you tell?"

Shane chuckled and Levi looked ready to laugh. "Hey, Unc, can I go out tonight? It's Friday night."

Levi looked startled by the question. "Where and with who?"

"A bunch of guys from school. They're picking me up at six and we're going to grab something to eat and then catch a movie."

"I guess so, as long as you're home by eleven."

"Eleven? How about midnight?"

"How about ten?"

"Eleven's cool." Shane glanced at the barn. "You want me to finish what I was doing yesterday?"

"Go ahead," Levi said. "I'll be right there."

She and Levi watched as Shane headed for the barn. As the boy disappeared inside she asked, "Would you like to come to dinner tonight?"

"What time?"

"Is six-thirty okay?" She couldn't bring herself to meet his gaze.

"Fine. Do you want me to bring anything?"

She shook her head and stepped up onto the porch. Opening the front door, she took a deep breath, gathered her courage, and said over her shoulder, "No, Levi, just come prepared."

EIGHT

Levi parked his truck in Georgia's driveway and turned off the ignition. He sat there and stared at his hands as they clutched the steering wheel. They were trembling. His fingers were actually shaking! He needed to get hold of himself before he saw Georgia. The woman had only invited him to dinner. Well, that wasn't the truth. They both knew what was on the menu for dessert.

They were mature, consenting adults who had their minds, as well as their eyes, wide open. So why did he feel as if he were letting her down? Letting himself down?

Georgia deserved candlelight and a meal she hadn't prepared herself. A romantic weekend in the Poconos or down the shore would have been better. A night at the local Holiday Inn would be more romantic than his rushing through dinner, carrying her upstairs, and ravishing her until ex-

actly ten forty-two, when he would have to leave
to beat Shane home for his eleven o'clock curfew.

He couldn't do this. Oh, physically he wanted
to in the worst way, but it just seemed so . . .
cheap? No, cheap wasn't the right word. Maybe
tawdry was the word he was looking for. The
whole thing reminded him of some shameful affair, done in secrecy. Done in the dark behind
locked doors. He wasn't ashamed of Georgia or
what he felt for her. He didn't particularly want
to broadcast it to the neighbors, the town, or especially to Shane, because he considered it in bad
taste and disrespectful to Georgia. Still, she deserved to be courted with flowers and champagne.
She deserved to be seen in public with him. She
deserved more than a one-night, one-week, or a
one-month stand.

Georgia De Witt was the kind of woman who
deserved white lace, a gold band, and the promise
of forever.

He got out of the truck, slammed the door,
and muttered a curse dark enough to entitle him
to burn in the fires of hell for a good portion of
eternity. Sometimes a strong religious upbringing
had its drawbacks. Muttering "sugar" or "fudge"
just didn't relieve all the frustrations.

He should be getting back in his truck and
driving as far and as fast as he could away from
Georgia. She was all wrong for him. Especially
now with Shane entering his life and turning it
upside down. The one thing he had always

wanted was a family. So now that he finally had one in the form of a definitely unconventional son, why wasn't he satisfied? He glanced at Georgia's welcoming house and knew why. Somewhere in the back of his stubborn and old-fashioned mind he wanted it all. He wanted a wife to go along with his son. After kissing Georgia, no one else would do.

He was in deep trouble now. He never should have connected Georgia and "wife" in the same thought. Now that that association had been made, it was going to be pure hell to sever it within his mind.

The green front door stood between him and Georgia. All he had to do was knock. He had knocked plenty of times on that door. So why did it seem so different this time? Hell, he even had Georgia's spare key to use in case she wasn't home and he needed to use the facilities or the phone. Georgia was entirely too trusting and tonight was entirely too personal. He took a deep breath, reached out, and knocked.

An hour later Levi wasn't sure if he had misread the invitation or if Georgia had changed her mind. Seduction hadn't been on the menu, pork chops and mashed potatoes had, along with applesauce and green beans. "That was delicious." He gave his stomach an extravagant pat to emphasize the point. "I didn't realize you were such a good cook." Truth be told, he had her pegged as a dine-out sort of person. He pictured her dining in the fanciest restaurants, eating food that he could barely pronounce. Tonight's meal, while not being a culinary masterpiece, had been both delicious and filling. His kind of meal.

"Thank you." She took the empty plate he had carried over to her and placed it in the dishwasher. "I hope you saved room for dessert."

His glance automatically slid down the length of her body. She had changed out of the jeans and T-shirt she'd had on earlier and into a flowing dark green calf-length skirt with sunflowers printed around the bottom. A golden blouse and a vest printed with the same sunflowers completed the outfit. She looked as if she belonged on the cover of *Country Miss* magazine, selling fresh air, apple pies, and sunshine. She wasn't dressed for seduction.

He turned his glance to the countertops, looking for the apple pie. "What are we having?"

"Apple dumplings."

He smiled. Close enough. "I guess I could manage to find room for one." He would rather eat apple dumplings with Georgia than get seduced by any other woman. Georgia had a way of lighting up a room with just her presence. She made everyone feel special, as if they had done something remarkable just by being there and showing up in her life. She charmed deliverymen with a smile and a friendly offer of something cold to drink. She'd had the two men who had delivered the kitchen cabinets tripping over their tongues and thinking they were gods. Even Shane, who connected with no one, was wrapped around her little finger. The amazing part was she hadn't a clue about the effect she had on the male population.

He walked back to the table to get the crystal dish containing the applesauce and the empty bowl the mashed potatoes had been in. What a difference between Georgia's idea of setting a table and what his wife used to do. Christine never scooped the applesauce from the jar, and the instant mashed potatoes she plopped down on the table were always served in the same pan they had been made in. The few pieces of crystal they had received as wedding presents never left the corner cabinet where they waited for that "special" meal that never materialized. Christine hated to cook.

He picked up the remaining dishes from the table and carried them over to Georgia, who was efficiently putting everything away. He didn't want to think about Christine or the way things had turned out between them. He'd much rather concentrate on Georgia and the fact that she had been gone for three days. "How did the trip to Kentucky go? Find anything interesting?"

"It went real well." She smiled at him as she reached up to the third shelf and pulled down a plastic bowl and lid. "I attended five different sales and managed to practically fill the rental truck out back."

"Why haven't you emptied the truck yet? Do you need any help?" She usually had the truck emptied and returned the same day she came home.

"No, I wasn't due back until late today. The man I hired to move furniture and empty trucks for the shops had the day off. He'll be there tomorrow morning to unload it for me."

"What time did you get home last night?" Shane and he had worked until seven, and she hadn't been back when they left.

"It wasn't last night, it was early this morning." She sealed the container holding the leftover green beans and placed it in the refrigerator. "Somewhere around four."

"In the morning!" What had she done, driven straight through the night? No wonder he hadn't seen her until sometime after eleven that morning.

"Last I looked, four A.M. was four in the morning."

She placed the platter the pork chops had been on inside the dishwasher and gave him a look that clearly warned him off any lecture he might have on his tongue. It was a real shame he never paid much attention to warnings. "Please don't tell me you were stupid enough to drive straight through the night."

Georgia's eyes narrowed to tiny slits and her

hands balled up into tight fists. "Fine, I won't tell you."

He was in trouble now, but he still couldn't drop the issue. She could have been molested at truck stops, hijacked, or involved in an accident. She could have fallen asleep behind the wheel and ended up in some ditch unnoticed for hours. She could have been lying there hurt and bleeding, or even killed. Thinking of the things that could have happened to a lone woman driving in the dead of night was enough to give him indigestion. Thinking of those things happening to Georgia was enough to give him an ulcer.

He had always considered Georgia an intelligent woman. Now he wasn't too sure. "Don't you realize what could have happened to you?"

She stood her ground and faced him down. "Don't you realize that it's not any of your business?"

"You're absolutely right, Georgia. It shouldn't be any of my business." He took a couple of steps toward her and backed her up against the counter. The fiery sparks of anger disappeared from her eyes, replaced with confusion. Good! If he had to go around in a state of confusion, he wanted someone with him.

He placed his hands on the counter, one on either side of her, but he didn't touch her. The sweet scent of her flowery perfume teased his senses and her luscious lips looked moist and inviting. He pulled his gaze away from her tempting mouth and met her eyes. "So what's a person to do if they care about you, Georgia? Pretend it doesn't matter if you foolishly drive hundreds of miles in the dead of the night?"

"I don't like pretenders, Levi."

"Good, I don't like to pretend." He moved a fraction of an inch closer. "So that leaves me caring about what happens to you."

She worried her lower lip for a moment without breaking eye contact. "You do?"

"Why else would I be here?" She didn't have to appear so damned shocked by his concern. Surely she'd had boyfriends in the past who'd cared about her. Her brother obviously cared about her. Levi had been surprised Morgan hadn't run a police check on him before allowing Georgia to hire him to work on her home and shop. Morgan looked like a man who would rip anyone apart who harmed his little sister. "Does your brother know you travel alone and at night?"

"Morgan knows I travel."

"That wasn't what I asked, Georgia, and you know it." He studied her face. If she wanted to keep the fact that she traveled alone and at night from her brother, that was her choice. But she wasn't going to keep it from him. He reached out and gently stroked the dark circles beneath her eyes. Makeup had done a wonderful job concealing them from him today, but at this distance, even makeup couldn't hide them. "You look exhausted."

"I don't sleep much when I'm on the road." She tried to turn her head away, but he cupped her chin and held her in place.

"Why not?"

"I don't like staying in strange motel rooms and I especially don't like sleeping in strange beds. I like being at home."

"Enough to risk driving hundreds of miles at night?"

"Yes."

If nothing else, he had to admire her conviction. Yelling at her wasn't going to change her mind. He wasn't sure if anything could. Georgia obviously was a homebody. She liked being at home. "You shouldn't push yourself so hard."

She chuckled. "You of all people should know how much hard work it is to get a business started and then to keep it going. If my calculations are correct, you average about sixty-five to seventy hours a week working here."

"And how many hours a week do you work?"

"Not that many."

"Add them up, Georgia. You might be surprised." He frowned at the dark circles and the fatigue pulling at her mouth. "You need to get some rest."

She gave him an impish smile. "Are you trying to tell me it's time for bed?"

Desire exploded in his gut and a stream of

heat pooled in his groin. The woman was too dangerous for his peace of mind. She needed to get some rest, not play adult games between the sheets. "I said, *you* need to get some rest."

She glanced at the clock and frowned. "It's only eight o'clock. If I go to sleep now I'll be up before dawn." She pouted and wrapped her arms around his neck as he tried to take a step back. "Aren't you in the mood for dessert?"

"I'll eat the apple dumpling tomorrow, okay?"

She reached up and brushed her mouth across his. "Who's talking about apple dumplings, Levi?"

"Come on, Georgia, I'm trying to be a gentleman here and let you get some rest."

She nipped at his lip. "I don't recall asking you to be a gentleman, Levi." She arched her back and wiggled her hips against the front of his slacks. "You wanted me this morning. What happened?"

His hands left the counter to clutch her hips and hold her against him. Her eyes widened as she felt his need press against her abdomen. "Nothing happened, Georgia. I'm just as hard now as I was then." His hips thrust involuntarily against her softness. "Maybe harder."

"So why the attack of conscience?" Her fingers brushed back the wave of hair that fell across his forehead.

"Because once we go there, Georgia, there will be no turning back. You'll be mine."

Her smile captured his heart and shattered his resistance. "I'm counting on it."

Georgia felt herself being picked up and hauled against his chest. Levi captured her mouth in a kiss that stole not only her breath, but her soul. She clung to his wide shoulders as he carried her out of the kitchen and up the stairs.

One thought permeated her mind: It was about damn time! For a while there in the kitchen she thought she would actually have to beg him to make love to her.

She felt the bounce of every step beneath her and the heat of Levi's hands as they cradled her thighs and back. She met the gentle riposte of his tongue and engaged it in a dance as old as time. His tame thrusts turned wild and demanding as he entered her bedroom and stood next to her antique sleigh bed.

He slowly ended the kiss and stood her on her feet. She blinked at the loss of heat and glanced around. Late evening light was still fingering its way in through the lace curtain. Shadows stretched across the room, touching the ivory satin comforter and painting a lacy pattern across Levi's face. She reached up and touched his smooth jaw, where he must have shaved before coming to dinner. "I want you to know the same thing holds true for me, Levi."

"About?" He turned his head and pressed a kiss into her palm.

"I care about you too." She could have added

a couple other declarations to that statement, but didn't. This was all too new, too fragile. She didn't want to frighten Levi with her feelings, but more important, she didn't want to frighten herself. She could examine her feelings later. For now she just wanted to experience the passion. For now she just wanted to want, wanted to need.

She opened her hand and cupped his jaw once again. "I want what your kisses started." Her fingers undid the first button on his shirt. "I want that promise of passion that is burning in your eyes." The next two buttons came undone. She smiled at the low moan that escaped him and stepped out of her sandals. "Can you give me that?"

She could only describe his grin as "wicked" as he carefully pushed her vest down her arms. The brightly printed material ended up on the floor. "I can give you all that and more."

She smiled as she spread his unbuttoned shirt wide and stroked her fingers up his chest. Soft dark curls wrapped around her fingers and she gave them a playful tug. "I don't know if I can handle more."

His shirt was a khaki and brown plaid, not his usual work shirt, and his pants were a khaki cotton twill, not his standard jeans. He had looked relaxed, confident, and in control all during dinner. It had been driving her out of her mind. She knew why she'd invited him to dinner, and in the secret corner of her naughty fantasies she had been hoping the pork chops would have turned to dust before they remembered to eat. So much for fantasies. The reality, though, was pretty terrific.

Levi's mouth skimmed down the side of her throat as his fingers inched her blouse upward. He pulled back as he tugged the blouse over her head and dropped it to the floor. Then his mouth settled over hers and she felt the button on her skirt come undone. The silk skirt slid down her legs, and she was picked up and tenderly deposited in the center of the bed.

She reached out a hand toward Levi, who was standing there staring at her as if he were in a trance. Self-conscious at lying across the bed with only a lacy bra and panties on, she started to worry. "Is something wrong?"

He slowly shook his head. "Wrong? What could possibly be wrong?" He kicked off his shoes and tugged off his socks. "You're the most beautiful woman I've ever seen."

She relaxed slightly. He wasn't leaving. She smiled, admiring his bare torso. "You have an incredible chest." If she were a sculptress, she would mold that magnificent work of human muscle out of clay so she could gaze at it any time she liked. As it was, she couldn't mold a salad bowl even if the clay came with directions. So she would just have to content herself with the real thing and commit it to memory.

She continued to smile as a flush swept up Levi's face, and he quickly finished disrobing and joined her on the bed. She couldn't tell if he had been embarrassed by her remark about his chest or if he was flustered undressing in front of her. From the quick look she had of his body, the man had absolutely no reason to be flustered.

He leaned on one elbow and gazed down at her. His fingers toyed with the lace edging of her bra. "Do you know how many nights I dreamed about joining you in your old-fashioned bed?"

"Not as many as I dreamed about having you here." She caressed his chest with the tips of her fingers. His arousal was pressing insistently against her hip. Her hand slid downward and his thickness jerked upward in response. He seemed to be reaching for her touch, stretching, growing. . . . Her fingers trembled with anticipation.

His hand shot out and captured hers. His breathing was jerky and harsh. "Not yet."

"Why? Haven't we waited long enough?"

He brought her hand up and placed it on his shoulder. His nice safe shoulder. "After all the wait, I would like this to last longer than two minutes." He unclasped the front catch of her bra and slowly peeled it away, then placed a fleeting kiss on each nipple.

She felt her insides dissolve with those kisses. She wanted more. She wanted to feel Levi everywhere. "It's like a roller coaster. First you stand in line waiting an incredibly long time, all the while anticipating the ride. Then once you're strapped into the seat it's over in a blink of an eye and you haven't even had time to catch your breath."

Levi bent down, and this time he sucked each berry-hard nipple deep inside his mouth, then released them and lavished each one with a swift stroke of his tongue. "Do you like roller coasters, Georgia?"

She smiled as she pulled his head up to her waiting mouth. He understood her need. There would be time later for a slow, romantic journey through the "Tunnel of Love." Now she needed the passion, not the finesse. "I love them." She met his kiss with everything she had and was rewarded with his feverish groan and hands that swept away the remaining scraps of silk. They were flesh to flesh, each touching anywhere they could reach.

Heat erupted wherever he touched. Her breasts ached when he left them to skim lower. Her abdomen trembled from the warmth of his fingers and mouth. Thighs instinctively parted, impatient for his touch. His strong, sure fingers coaxed her to the brink, only to bring her back, then propel her higher than before. With each thrust of his finger, she was going mad with desire. She had never been this high, this wound up. She felt like a tightly coiled spring, ready to detonate.

Her hands clutched his buttocks and urged him to put an end to her madness. She wanted to feel the length, the thickness, the heat of him inside her. Her moan of despair filled the room as he pushed himself off her and the bed. Her hand reached out blindly. "Levi?"

"Sh. . . ." He dug into his pants pocket and the sound of ripping foil, followed by her sigh of relief, echoed in the room. "I'm right here."

She smiled into the dusk-filled room. Everything was in shadows now. She started at the feel of Levi's mouth against her ankle. "What are you doing?" From her position, she could only see the top of his head.

"Working my way up to heaven." His lips skimmed her calf and teased the inside of her knee.

"Oh, my!" She clutched the satin comforter as his tongue stroked her inner thigh. Her hips rose off the bed as he pierced the moist threshold his fingers had so skillfully prepared. The brink was within her reach, she was going to fall . . . "Levi!"

He moved up her body to tug each nipple into his mouth. She clutched at his hair and forced him upward. Her thighs were wrapping around his hips and she could feel his heavy thickness poised at her opening. She arched upward and he penetrated deeply with one thrust.

Levi threw back his head and held his body still in rigid control, as if he were waiting for her to adjust to his invasion. She reached up and placed a handful of kisses along his throat, wherever she could reach. "It's fine, Levi." She tightened her thighs and pulled him in deeper to prove her point.

He groaned and stared at her. "It's more than just fine. It's heaven." His mouth swooped down and the dance began. Breaths grew rapid, skin turned slippery, and the rhythm quickened with each thrust.

She clutched his shoulders and hung on for dear life. She'd never experienced anything like this before. The brink was directly in front of her, then it rose, and then rose some more. She reached blindly for the edge as she rode the storm named Levi. She could see the control he was trying to exert over his body. He had found the edge with her and was masterfully holding on until she was ready.

Two more thrusts and she could go no higher. She gripped Levi harder and shouted his name as the brink disappeared beneath her feet and her world shattered.

Her name was torn from his throat as he matched her climax with his own.

Two hours later Georgia found herself in the same satisfied condition. Only this time she was lying in bed the right way and Levi was cradling her in his arms. Their second journey had started out slow and incredibly sweet, but the results had been the same as their first voyage. Total wild abandonment, but she wasn't complaining.

Levi turned his head and glanced at the clock on the nightstand. "I have to be going if I want to be home before Shane." He kissed the top of her head. "I don't want him to come home to a totally dark house."

She snuggled her cheek against his chest. She didn't want him to go, but she understood. Shane was a confused sixteen-year-old kid who'd just lost his parents. She, on the other hand, was a mature, well-adjusted adult who had gotten more than she had bargained for with Levi. "I'll walk you to the door." The last thing she wanted to do was to get up. She felt as if every one of her bones had turned into noodles. Soggy, overcooked noodles.

Levi raised her face and kissed her deeply. "You are to stay in bed and get some sleep." He trailed his kiss to her ear and playfully nipped at the lobe. "I want to dream about you just as you are; naked and wearing the most satisfied expression on your face."

"I've got to lock the doors."

"I have a key." He kissed her one last time before sliding out from under the sheet. "Sleep in tomorrow morning and I'll see you when you wake up."

She muffled her yawn with the pillow. She was so tired, nothing was making sense. Except Levi's leaving. That she understood. "You will?"

He tugged up his pants and reached for his shirt. "It's Saturday." He sat on the side of the bed and pulled on his socks and shoes. "Remember I'm working for you."

She snuggled deep into the pillow. "In that case, you can sleep in tomorrow too." Her voice faded into the downy softness.

Levi finished dressing while staring at the sleeping woman. She didn't even stir when he leaned over and kissed her cheek. With great tenderness, he brushed a strand of golden hair away from her lips and tucked it behind her ear. "Sleep well, love." He stood up, released a heavy sigh, and left the room.

NINE

Levi was beginning to feel like a fool. He had spent the first hour and a half that Saturday morning working on the outside of the barn. The side closest to the house. After every two swings of his hammer he had glanced over at the house to see if there was any sign of Georgia. It was just after eight and he hadn't seen her. The only thing he had received so far was a string of smart aleck "know-it-all" looks from Shane and a crick in his neck.

With one last glance at the house he headed for the back of the barn and entered the lower level, where Shane was working. The old support posts of the barn were in excellent shape, but he wanted to add a few more to help with the weight they'd be adding to the loft. Shane was trying to dig six one-foot round, three-foot deep footers to serve as the base of the new posts. "How's it going?" It didn't look as if his nephew were making much headway, and the cement truck was scheduled for first thing Monday morning.

"The dirt is packed so tight, it's like trying to dig through solid rock." Shane wiped his forearm across his brow and left a streak of dirt behind.

Levi examined the hole Shane had been working on. "That's because for the last century people, farm equipment, and livestock have been packing it down." He shook his head at the shovel his nephew was holding. "You'll never get anywhere with that." He walked over to the side of the barn, where he had placed an assortment of digging instruments, and selected a pick. "Stand back and let an old man show you how to do it."

Shane grinned and stepped to the side. "Just don't have a heart attack on me, old man. My CPR is rusty."

He matched the boy's grin with one of his own. The way he was feeling this morning, he could dig his way to China without working up a sweat. He hadn't felt this good in years. Hell, he had never felt this good. He raised the pick over his shoulder and took a mighty swing. Hard, packed dirt flew in every direction.

Twenty minutes later, two of the holes were nearly done. With him manning the pick and Shane working the shovel they made an impressive team. They worked in companionable silence, and for the first time since seeing Shane at the airport Levi felt hope. The previous night

Shane had returned home with exactly one minute to spare, and his two friends had come into the house with him. They seemed like nice boys, and if the amount of soda and chips they had devoured was any indication, they were perfectly normal and healthy. Levi was thrilled that Shane had made a couple of friends and had even agreed to extend his curfew to eleven-thirty tonight when he went out again.

Levi walked over to where the next hole was marked out, lifted the pick, and took a powerful swing. Chunks of dried dirt flew everywhere.

"Geez . . . " cried Georgia as she brushed off the front of her jeans. "You guys should warn a person before she enters a room." She picked two dirt flakes from her shirt and frowned. "Please tell me it's only dirt flying around in here."

Shane laughed. "Morning, George. Don't worry, Unc would rather wear a dress on the job site than chuck cow turds at his boss."

Levi looked at Georgia and grinned. "I don't know about that one, it would have to depend on what type of dress." She looked adorable, sexy, and totally flustered.

She was dressed in a pair of jeans that had to have been made just to drive him crazy. Soft, worn denim caressed her legs as only a lover should. She was also wearing a red polo shirt with the logos from her other two stores printed in white just above the left breast. *A Touch of Home* and *Home Fires* couldn't have received better publicity. He had to wonder how she was going to fit the name of her new shop, *Heart and Home*, onto the shirt. Huge printing across the back of a shirt wasn't Georgia's style.

He glanced at the logos once more and realized that all three of Georgia's stores had the word "home" in them. For being such an independent, self-supporting, unattached woman it seemed an odd coincidence.

Georgia winked at Shane. "A kilt. Definitely a kilt."

"I'm not Scottish, nor do I have red hair. I'm one hundred percent Pennsylvania Dutch and proud of it." He didn't like the gleam in Georgia's eyes as she checked out his body. He especially didn't like his body's reaction to her scrutiny.

"Neither was Mel Gibson when he starred in that movie, *Braveheart*, a couple years ago." Georgia grinned. "All I kept thinking throughout that entire movie was what in the world was he wearing underneath that plaid and where was a good blustery storm when you needed one."

Shane took one look at his uncle's face and busted up laughing. "You won't have to wait for a breeze, George. All you'll have to do is stand at the bottom of a ladder."

Levi didn't mind being the butt of their joke, but he would rather they focus on something besides what he would or would not have on under a kilt. "If you two are done making fun of my lack of Scottish heritage, maybe you can try the pick for a turn, Shane." He looked at Georgia, wanting to remove that silly grin from her lips and replace it with something else, like his mouth. He was dying to kiss her good morning. Morning afters were hard enough, he didn't want Shane witnessing theirs. "I take it you're getting ready to head on down to the shops to empty the truck?"

"Yes. I just stopped in to see if you two needed anything before I left."

"We're fine." He nodded at the hole he had just started. "Try the pick on that one, Shane, while I walk Georgia to the truck."

"Gotcha, boss man," Shane said. "Bye, George."

"Bye, Seaweed."

"You can call me Shane now." Shane wouldn't meet Georgia's or Levi's gaze. He looked at the pick clutched in his hands instead. "Some memories should be held in real tight so you don't lose them." He glanced up and winked at Georgia. "Besides, babes might not appreciate going out with a guy whose name sounds like pond scum."

Georgia winked back. "True, but one piece of advice, don't refer to girls as 'babes.' It might be just as big a turnoff as pond scum."

"Cool rule, George."

"You're welcome." Georgia turned to the door and walked out into the sunlight with Levi.

The yellow rental truck was parked in front of the garage. They walked across the green slope of lawn in silence. When they were far enough away from the barn that Levi was pretty sure Shane couldn't see them, he reached for her hand and pulled her around the side of the truck, where he was positive Shane couldn't see them. Instantly, he captured her mouth in a heated kiss. Long moments went by before he could bring himself to end the kiss. Georgia tasted like minty toothpaste and coffee.

He smiled down at her as he cupped her bottom and pressed her against his arousal. It was a useless action because there was nothing he could do about it, but he wanted her to know how much he still wanted her. Georgia's desirability was very important to her. "Good morning."

Her hands were wrapped around his neck, and she was playing with the ends of his hair. "Wow. You can say good morning to me like that every morning."

He chuckled with relief. He hadn't been sure how she was going to handle this change in their relationship, but she appeared to have adjusted to it just fine. "How did you sleep?"

"Like a rock." She toyed with his ear, before lowering her fingers to play with the buttons on his shirt. "I should have left here forty minutes ago, but it seems I forgot to set the alarm last night."

"You must have been thinking about something else." He reached for her wandering hand and clasped it against his chest. If she wandered any lower, there was no way he would allow her to get into the truck and drive away.

"I don't know what that could have been," she teased. "It was a pretty uneventful evening."

He could see the laughter gleaming in her eyes. *"Uneventful!"* He tightened his hold on her hips and hauled her in closer. His mouth brushed her cheek and was slowly making its way to her tempting mouth. "I'll give you uneventful."

"Promises, promises." She stood on her toes and met his mouth.

This kiss lasted longer than the first one had, and it created more heat. More frustration. He pulled himself away, and this time he took a step back. "You're a very dangerous woman, Georgia De Witt."

She seemed surprised by his statement. "I am?"

"There isn't another woman alive who could get me away from my work and make me want to play all day." He tenderly brushed her cheek. "It's a good thing it's Saturday and Shane's here, or there's no telling what we'd be doing this very minute."

"Makes a person wish it were Monday, doesn't it?"

He chuckled, but took another step back just to be safe. "Like I said, Georgia, you're dangerous."

She smiled as if he had just paid her the most precious compliment in the whole world. "Speaking of Shane, how did it go last night?"

"He seems to have made some friends." Levi breathed a sigh of relief at the change of topics. "I met two of them last night, and they seem like okay kids. They dressed weird, said some stuff that I had no idea what they were referring to, and drank every drop of soda in the house."

"Sounds like normal teenagers to me."

"He's going out again tonight with them. They're taking him to the mall in Lancaster to do some shopping, then they're renting a movie and watching it at one of the kids' houses." He glanced at the barn where his nephew was working and prayed he was doing the right thing by allowing him this much freedom. "He's got to be in by eleven-thirty."

"Relax, Levi. It sounds like typical teenage stuff to me."

"I know, but how do you know if you're giving them too much freedom, or not enough?" He gave a heavy sigh at the complexities of raising a teenager.

"Shane will be fine. He looks as if he can take care of himself, and you did say you met the other boys."

"You're right. Why borrow trouble?" He lightly tugged on her ponytail. "Speaking of trouble, what are you doing tonight?"

"I thought about riding around and looking

for men wearing kilts, but I heard they're pretty rare in this county."

"Would you settle for dinner and a movie?"

She smiled up at him. "I thought you'd never ask."

Georgia nestled deeper into Levi's embrace. A late summer breeze was teasing the lace curtains, hinting at autumn's impending arrival. Her bed was the perfect place for snuggling after a hastily eaten dinner and a round of long leisurely love-making, compliments of Levi. She hadn't performed too shabbily herself if Levi's still erratic breathing was any indication.

She walked her fingers up his chest, toying with a curl here and there as she went. "You do know how to perk up a Thursday night."

His chuckle vibrated beneath her cheek. "Hey, you were the one to invite me to dinner."

"You were the one who wanted dessert when I offered."

"How was I supposed to know you would plop your butt on the kitchen table and start unbuttoning your blouse?" His hands softly stroked her back and hip.

She rubbed her thigh against his hip and smiled against his chest at his response. They had been lovers for nearly a week, and he still amazed her every time he responded to her simplest of touches. She had the power to arouse him, just as he held the capacity to make her melt with only a look. "You have something against the way I serve dessert?"

Levi heaved himself up, and two seconds later she found herself pinned under his body. His big, strong, partially aroused body. "We were damn lucky to make it upstairs." He pressed his mouth against the side of her neck where her pulse was pounding with renewed desire. "Next time give a man some warning, will you?"

She arched her neck to give him better access. "I'll think about it."

He rolled his weight again, bringing her with him so she was once again lying across his chest. "I know I come from generations of sturdy stock, but could you give me a minute to catch my breath?"

She nudged his semihard arousal with her thigh. "Fine, we'll talk about your sturdy stock later. What do you want to talk about? Shane, the skylights, how about the weather?"

"How about the fair?"

"What fair?" She lightly scraped her fingernail over his left nipple and was fascinated by the way it puckered.

"The Denver Fair. The one Shane's at tonight with a bunch of kids from school."

She pressed her mouth to his other nipple and ran her tongue over the nub. It too sprang to life. "I vote for them to continue the fair until sometime in November."

Levi playfully slapped her on her bottom. "Brat." He captured her wandering hand. "I was wondering if you wanted to go tomorrow night?"

"To the fair?"

"No, to the moon." He raised his hand to give her another pat, but ended up squeezing her instead. "Of course, to the fair. Everyone goes to the Denver Fair. It's the only proper thing to do when you live in Denver."

"I live in Reinholds."

"But my mailing address is Denver. So will you come with me?"

"Will there be food?" She brought their connected hands to her mouth. "I keep inviting you to dinner, and we get very little eating done." She took a tiny nip out of his thumb.

"There'll be plenty of food." He yanked his hand away before she could get in a second nip. "Enough to satisfy even your appetite."

She grinned wickedly as she surveyed his body. "Really?"

"Behave yourself. Shane and his friends will probably be there. It must be the 'in' place to hang."

"Do they still use the word 'in'?"

"No, I think I heard them referring to it as 'scoping for babes.'"

"I warned him about using that word. He's going to regret it one of these days."

"Shane wasn't the one who said it. I think it was his friend Chad."

She settled back down next to Levi and rested her head on his shoulder. "He's changed a lot in the past week, hasn't he?"

"I gather you're referring to Shane and his new haircut."

"I think he looks cute with all that peach fuzz all over his head." Monday night Shane had stopped at the local barber's and had his spikes buzzed off. His hair was now all one length—short. Incredibly short. "I was referring to his attitude too. He seems calmer, more accepting." She nestled closer. "I think he knows about our seeing each other."

"Count on it." Levi turned and placed a kiss on top of her head. "I told him. I didn't want him to find out from someone else. Since I'm not planning on sneaking around with you and we might end up at the same place as him and his friends, it seemed logical that I tell him."

She nervously bit her lip. Shane was Levi's family. "How did he take the news?"

"He said it was cool, and that you were one fine-looking babe-o-rama." Levi wiggled his eyebrows as his gaze slid to her breasts pressing against his chest. "I hate to tell you this, Georgia, but I have to agree with the boy. You are one fine-looking babe-o-rama."

She tried to stop the blush sweeping up her cheeks, but failed miserably. Levi sounded sincere and she wanted to believe him so desperately.

He cupped her chin and raised her face.

"What's the matter, Georgia? I didn't mean it disrespectfully. It's just that I happen to agree with my nephew, you're one very beautiful lady."

She tried to turn her head so he wouldn't notice the tears forming in her eyes. "What time did you say you had to be home by?" It was barely nine.

Levi kept his grip on her chin. "Talk to me, Georgia. Why do you get all flustered whenever I pay you a compliment?" His thumb caressed her cheek. "It's almost as if you're afraid to believe them."

She didn't know how to respond to that, so she just blinked back tears and stared at him.

"Surely other men have told you how beautiful you are?"

"In the social circle my brother and sometimes I myself have to travel in, compliments are about as trustworthy as politicians' promises." She shrugged. "In my book, actions speak louder than words."

"Don't you like the country club scene?"

"Not necessarily. I play Morgan's hostess when the need arises, but that's about it now." She managed to tuck her head back into the nice comfortable crevice between his neck and shoulder.

She went on. "My college sweetheart used to pay me outrageous compliments all the time, and I was naive enough to believe them. It turned out he was after the De Witt fortune and figured the easiest way to it was through me."

Levi stiffened beneath her. "Nice guy."

"Hmmm . . . " She reached for his hand and intertwined their fingers. "My second lover entered my life when I was twenty-six. He filled my head with pretty speeches and flowery promises while he was trying to figure out how to empty my savings account into his so he could continue to play the tables in Atlantic City. Morgan caught on to him before I did, and he took care of the problem."

"That's two thank-yous that I owe your brother."

She squeezed his hand. "You already know about Adam and our broken engagement."

"Yeah, a real sweetheart of a guy."

"It wasn't his fault that he fell in love with another woman. They were married a couple of weeks ago." She smiled at Levi. "I even went to the wedding."

"God, Georgia. You really know how to pick them."

She had to frown at that comment. "Yeah, I guess I do." Her gaze caressed his handsome face, and she wondered if she was going to regret taking Levi into her bed.

"Adam is a good guy, Levi. He wasn't after anything besides a wife. He didn't make any false promises. In fact, he didn't even break my heart, and I guess that makes me the weak one. I should have called off the wedding. How could I have contemplated marrying a man I didn't love, and who didn't love me back?"

"Maybe it was . . . you know . . . lust?"

The last word seemed to have been torn from his throat. "Lust? No. You see, that's what had me so upset at the time. There was no lust. We were never lovers. Hell, we never even got to first base."

"Never?"

"I think I would have remembered if we had, Levi. Adam didn't desire me, and the two lovers from my past wanted my bank account, not me. So . . . "

"You think I'm sleeping with you for your bank account?"

"No." She shook her head. "I know you're not after my money; that never entered my head." She didn't want Levi to think that for one moment. "Before you came into my life, I thought there was something wrong with me. Something that turned men off."

Levi burst out laughing. He shook the bed and her body as his mirth filled the room. "You thought there was something wrong with you? Are you out of your mind?"

She was relieved by his reaction, but did he really have to laugh so hard? The whole time she had been engaged to Adam she had questioned her sexuality, her lack of desire, Adam's lack of passion. His falling in love with another woman had only reinforced her fears. She lowered her gaze. "I'm sorry, Levi, I shouldn't have told—"

He cut her off before she could finish the sentence. Raising her head, he studied her face. "You're serious, aren't you?" He didn't wait for her answer. "Lord, Georgia, I'm sorry. I didn't mean to laugh." His mouth brushed her cheek. "It's just that you're so desirable and gorgeous that I couldn't imagine anyone, including yourself, thinking otherwise."

"Really?"

He kissed her lips. "Give me a half hour and I'll show you there's absolutely nothing wrong with you." His tongue teased the corner of her mouth. "Hell, give me a week and I'll be your slave for life."

Georgia held Levi's hand as they strolled the packed midway of the Denver Fair the next night. For being a small town fair, an awful lot of people, rides, food, and games were crammed into the park. Neon lights, loud voices, and the hum of generators filled the air, along with the tempting aroma of food. All kinds of delicious smelling foods. Sausages sizzling with peppers and onions, grilling hamburgers, french fries, and roasting beef were just a few she could pick out. Stands with hanging bags of cotton candy, stacks of red soda cups, and neat lines of candy apples were seen in every direction.

Vendors were hawking their wares while game operators dared you to try your luck at everything from darts, to water pistols, to tossing rolls of toilet paper into open toilets.

"Hungry yet?" Levi pulled her closer so a mother pushing a stroller with twins could get around her and over the maze of thick wires running everywhere.

"Starved." She glanced at the huge side of cooked beef at the local baseball team's booth, which was being sliced into thick roast beef sandwiches, and fairly drooled. "How about here?"

"Smells good to me." They wove their way to the booth and ordered two sandwiches and sodas. Levi passed Georgia her dinner and pocketed the change. "There's some picnic tables set up over there." He nodded past the carousal, the pink and blue flying elephant ride, and the ticket booth.

"Great." Georgia made her way to the only empty table and sat down. "This is terrific, Levi. Thanks." She took a bite out of the sandwich and glanced around at the wild assortment of people and activities. This was truly a country fair.

When they had first arrived they had toured the huge striped tents where the homegrown produce was displayed and ribbons marked the winners of each category. She still didn't have the foggiest notion what made one zucchini better than another, but row after row of vegetables, fruits, and even freshly cut flowers had been impressive. She had marveled at the largest pumpkin and smiled at the local kindergartner's attempts at painting faces on the orange pumpkins. Their second stop had been the arts and crafts display, along with the preserve competition in the recreation building.

Levi then had hauled her into the livestock tent where cute docile-looking sheep captured her heart. The sheer size of the cows left her leery. Cows always looked so unthreatening while grazing in the fields, but up close and personal was another story. She hadn't been swayed by their big brown eyes. Levi had thought her reaction to the cud-chewing heifers had been laughable.

She took another bite out of her sandwich and refused to think about what she was eating. Living on bean sprouts and broccoli for the rest of her life held no appeal.

A child's insistent cry had her looking to her left. She spotted the bawling baby immediately, but also saw someone else. Shane and a cute blond-haired girl were making their way toward them. She kicked Levi under the table.

"Hey," he protested.

She knew it wasn't much of a warning, but it was all she could think of to do. Shane looked nervous about the impending introductions. The girl looked as if she would rather climb into the cage with the five-foot-long, two-headed serpent advertised at the other end of the midway. "Hi, Shane."

Levi turned to the left and froze.

Shane frowned. "Unc, George, I would like you to meet Cynthia. She's in my science and math classes at school." Shane's arm stayed locked around the girl's shoulders. "Cynthia, I would like you to meet my uncle Levi and a friend of ours, Georgia De Witt."

Cynthia nodded. "Hi."

"Hello, Cynthia," Georgia said. "Nice to meet you." The girl looked as wholesome as buttermilk bread, from her perky ponytail to her designer jeans, fashionably baggy sweater and the windbreaker that proclaimed she was on the varsity cheerleading squad. No wonder Shane had been changing. He was smitten, and if Cynthia's obvious preference to stay glued to his side was any indication, so was she. They made a cute pair.

Georgia glanced at Levi, who still hadn't uttered one syllable. She saw Shane's stricken expression and kicked Levi again.

Levi glared at her before turning back to the young couple. "Hello, Cynthia." He looked at his nephew. "Do you need a ride home?"

"No, Cynthia has a car. She's giving me a lift."

"I want you in early tonight," Levi said.

"Why? You said I can stay out till eleven-thirty."

"We have a lot of work to get done tomorrow at Georgia's. I want to get an early start."

Shane's expression turned stubborn as he

glared at his uncle. "We'll get your early start, don't sweat it." He gave Georgia a fleeting smile. "Thanks, George. See you in the morning."

Without saying another word, Shane turned and walked away, dragging a confused and embarrassed-looking Cynthia with him.

Georgia turned and frowned at Levi, who was staring after the young couple. "Well, that was rude!"

"Back off, Georgia. It doesn't concern you."

He might as well have slapped her. *It doesn't concern you!* He couldn't have put it any plainer. Levi wasn't prepared to share his life. "I think it's time for you to take me home, Levi. I've suddenly developed a splitting headache." It wasn't a lie. A headache had formed at the base of her skull and the roast beef sandwich she had just eaten felt like a brick lying in her stomach. A huge, square-edged burning brick.

TEN

With each passing day Georgia became more confused. Whatever desire Levi had felt for her was surely dead. The man had barely looked at her, let alone spoken to her, in the past week. He had politely declined two dinner invitations with the excuse that Shane needed him at home. From the little she had seen of Levi and Shane working together during the past week, she would hazard a guess that the tension between the two stubborn males was worse now than it had been when the boy first arrived.

She could even go as far as pinpoint the exact time everything changed. The defining moment came while they were eating roast beef sandwiches at the fair and Shane had introduced them to his girlfriend, Cynthia. From that moment on, everything just fell apart. *Why*, she hadn't a clue. She couldn't figure out why Cynthia's appearance on the scene changed anything. Or even if it had been Cynthia that caused the change.

Shane was still being Shane, not the spiked-hair Seaweed. The bare-breasted mermaid hadn't made a return appearance. Nor had the dog collars or spiked wristband. The boy looked and acted as nearly normal as a teenage could get, and all Levi kept doing was riding him, riding him hard. The previous afternoon she had overheard their argument about Shane's going out that night. Levi had won. Shane had lost. And she had kept her nose out of it because it wasn't any of her business.

She couldn't think what she might have done to upset Levi at the fair besides point out his rudeness, and that was after the fact. The drive home that night had been strained, but blessedly short. She had gotten out of his truck, told him she didn't need to be seen to the door, and entered her house without a backward glance. Tears had been rolling down her cheeks before Levi's truck backed out of the driveway.

Levi had made it perfectly plain to her that she wasn't wanted or needed in his life. It was just so hard to accept that because she had come to realize how much she loved him and Shane. She had begun to picture them all as a family.

A knock on the patio doors had her turning toward them. Her heart cried for Levi, while her brain shouted for an Avon lady. A dejected-looking Shane stood on the other side of the screen door. Her heart went out to the young boy.

She slid open the door. "Come on in, Shane."

He wiped his feet and stepped into the kitchen. "Thanks. Levi just left for the hardware store."

She had been so deep in thought that she hadn't even heard the truck. "Would you like something to drink? How about a snack? I have some fresh fruit." She had just pulled up into the driveway half an hour earlier, the same time Shane was getting off the school bus. The boy had to be hungry. She picked up a fat shiny apple and tossed it to him.

"Thanks." Shane tossed the apple into the air and caught it again. His frown seemed to deepen. "I came to ask a favor of you, George."

"Name it." She had to smile at his astonished look. Obviously he wasn't used to unconditional acceptance. Over the past several weeks she had come to know Shane pretty well. She knew what he was going to ask for, before he even spoke. He wanted her to run interference with Levi for him.

"Something's bugging Levi and I don't know what it is. He's changed, and not for the better."

"I know. He's been awfully hard on you lately."

"You don't know half of it."

She raised her eyebrows at that. She only got to see Levi when he was working. He wasn't very communicative and he had the annoying habit of always being up some ladder whenever she was around. "What don't I know?"

"He won't let me out."

She blinked. "At all?"

"Last Sunday he came up with this brilliant idea, it's called family day. We spent the entire day visiting relatives I've never met before at the other end of the county." Shane made a face that clearly indicated his views on family day. "Monday night he allowed Chad and Wayne to come over and watch the football game with us. But every night since he's come up with one lame-brained excuse after another about why I can't go out."

"Have you gotten into trouble that I don't know about, or have you violated any curfews?" It was worse than she had thought. Levi was strangling Shane with his tight grip.

"No, I've been cool." He tossed the apple once again. "I was wondering if you would talk to him to see what his problem is. I asked him last night and he informed me he doesn't have a problem."

"What about Cynthia?"

"Cynthia?" He seemed startled by that question. "What's she got to do with any of this?"

"I'm not sure she does, but Levi's attitude changed the minute he met her at the fair." How was it possible for Shane to look more disheartened? "Do you think it's possible for Levi to know Cynthia or her family? Denver is still a relatively small town, where everyone knows everyone else."

"I doubt it. Cynthia and her family just moved here last winter. Her dad's some big shot over at the Pepperidge Farm factory and her mom's a nurse."

"Sounds like a nice family." She gazed out the door toward the barn. Her dream shop was coming along beautifully. It was a real shame her life wasn't so easily reconstructed. "I'll have a talk with Levi for you, but I have to warn you we haven't been getting along lately."

"At first I thought his problem was with you and he was just taking it out on me." Shane turned the apple in his hand and studied it from every angle. "Then I realized it was me he had the problem with, but for the life of me I can't figure out what I've done wrong." He flipped the apple high into the air and caught it. "Sorry, I guess I screwed up your life too."

She reached out and touched his arm. "No, Shane, it's not your fault. Whatever Levi's problem is you didn't cause it, Cynthia didn't cause it, and I didn't cause it. It's his problem." The poor kid had been through enough in the past year, and he didn't need any extra baggage. She was going to have a talk with Levi, and he wasn't going to like what she had to say.

Levi parked in front of the barn so he wouldn't have to walk near Georgia's house. The paper bag on the seat beside him was filled with the nails he needed. He was needing a lot of things in his life lately. He wished he could get them all by going to the local lumberyard.

He was losing Shane and he was helpless to prevent the inevitable. It was as if he were stuck in quicksand and life was slowly pulling him under. He knew he was being unreasonable with the boy, but he couldn't stop it. He was consumed with the fear that Shane was going to repeat his mistake with his high school sweetheart and have to get married.

When he took Shane into his life, it never dawned on him that the boy was the exact age Levi had been when he first started dating Christine. Hormones and sixteen were a deadly combination. Neither one of them made it out of the eleventh grade a virgin. He guessed he should be thankful they were a couple of years out of high school before she announced she was pregnant. At the time it had seemed like a sick coincidence that that announcement came just when he was realizing they both wanted something different from life.

Christine's clinging presence during his journey into adulthood had limited his choices. He didn't want Shane to suffer the same fate.

He had sat there at the picnic table in the middle of the fair, looking at his nephew with his arm around a cute young cheerleader, and he'd been struck by a foreboding sense of déjà vu. Christine had been a cheerleader with a perky blond ponytail and a killer smile. Shane's life had flashed before his eyes. It had paralleled his own.

Now he was stuck with that haunting image and he was inadvertently pushing Shane toward it.

And Georgia! He didn't even want to think what he had done to her. How could he have been so cruel as to tell her it wasn't any of her business? He knew how she felt toward Shane. His behavior was inexcusable, and he didn't have the guts to tell Georgia or Shane why he had acted as he had.

The only thing he could do was to avoid Georgia and her questioning glances. How could he, in good conscience, keep Shane from his girlfriend while dating Georgia? It would be like rubbing the kid's face in mud and then laughing at him. He couldn't do that to his nephew. So that meant he had to stop seeing Georgia. Lord, what a predicament!

It was pure torture, seeing her every day and not being able to hold her. He ached from not holding her. He made up excuses about why he didn't have the time to talk to her whenever she came into the barn. He taped notes to her door detailing the work and dreamed of her every night.

He gazed out the windshield and studied the barn. It was going to be one impressive-looking antique store by the time he and Georgia were done with it. He usually didn't take on such long-range jobs, but there was something special about Georgia and her dreams for the barn. He couldn't have refused the challenge to see that dream become a reality.

Now he was stuck working there till spring. Spring was one lonely cold autumn and winter away. With a weary sigh he reached for the bag of nails and got out of the truck.

He never made it to the barn door. Georgia waylaid him a good six feet from the entrance.

"Can I have a moment of your time, Levi?"

"Can't it wait? I want to finish framing out the powder room and office before I call it a night." He couldn't care less about framing the remaining walls, it was only an excuse. He didn't trust himself around Georgia. If he closed his eyes, he could still taste her, feel her heat surround him and bring him to a climax, time after time.

She stepped directly in front of him. "No, it can't wait." She raised her chin and silently dared him to argue. "It's about Shane."

He quickly stepped forward. "Is he hurt?" Why hadn't he thought about all the things that could injure an inexperienced sixteen-year-old boy? He'd never forgive himself if something happened to the kid.

"No, he's not hurt physically, but he's hurting, Levi." She still blocked his way. "He doesn't understand what he's being punished for."

"He's not being punished!" She was making

him sound like a monster, when all he was trying to do was give the kid a future.

"Shane thinks he is." Georgia crossed her arms. "So do I."

"Well, he's not!" He refused to meet her eyes. He wouldn't be able to handle the disgust he knew would be there. Disgust he didn't deserve. "Back off, Georgia." He had enough self-doubt, he didn't need to hear any more from her. "Shane's my family and I'll raise him the best way I know how."

Georgia visibly jerked at his verbal blow, but she held her ground. "You're making a mistake, Levi. You're going to lose him if you keep pushing him the way you are." She took a deep breath and pleaded, "Just talk to him. Tell him what's going through your mind."

He kept his gaze focused on the entrance of the barn. The pain in her voice was tearing him to shreds, and he knew he had just killed everything that had been between them. But Shane was his family, he had to come first. "What's going through my mind is work. I have a job to do and you're keeping me from it."

She stepped aside and fired off a parting shot. "Some people don't deserve children, Levi."

Her words hit a perfect bull's-eye. He didn't deserve Shane. He surely hadn't deserved sweet little Jenny, because if he had, wouldn't the blood tests have shown that he was her father?

❖———————❖

Georgia reached for the phone while trying to read the clock next to her bed. One-thirty in the morning! "Hello?" If this was a wrong number she would kill the idiot on the other end.

"Georgia, it's me, Levi. Sorry for disturbing you."

"Levi! What's wrong?" It didn't take a clear head to figure out something was seriously wrong for him to be calling at this hour.

"I thought you might want to know you were right."

She frowned at the phone, sat up farther, and leaned against the headboard. He didn't sound drunk, but there was an odd quality to his voice. "About what?"

"Shane took off." There was a funny sound, as if he were trying to control himself.

"Took off? Where?"

"He left a note on the kitchen table. It said, 'Hey, we tried.' He didn't even sign it. He lied to me this morning when he said he had to stay after school to catch up on some work."

"Are you telling me Shane ran away?" Memories of her argument with Levi two days ago came flooding back. She had predicted he was going to push the boy away, but she hadn't meant it. She had been hoping to snap Levi out of pulling the reins too tight on Shane.

"Looks that way," Levi said. "He didn't show

up for school today, and I've already checked at all his friends' houses. No one has seen him."

"What about Cynthia?"

"I was over there around nine. All she did was cry. She's afraid Shane will head back to Iowa and she'll never see him again."

Georgia rubbed her forehead and stared out the window. It was pitch dark, and somewhere out there was Shane. "Do you think he'd head for Iowa?" From what little she knew about Shane's past, she doubted it, but who knew what a sixteen-year-old thought. Her guess would be that he wouldn't travel too far from Cynthia. Love, even puppy love, was a powerful bond.

"I don't know." There was a long pause before he asked, "You didn't see him this evening, did you?"

"I would have told you if I had." She pulled up her knees and rested her chin on them. They had certainly reached a sorry state. A sixteen-year-old boy was alone out in the world, and the man she loved thought she would hide information from him. "Have you called the police?"

"Yes, they took down some information and are going to be keeping an eye out for him. The officer seems to think since he's only been here for such a short time he'll probably head back to Iowa."

Made sense to her, but she still didn't think it was right. "What are you going to do now? I

could get dressed and we could ride around looking for him."

"In the dark? We'd have better luck spotting
Santa. The officer said the best thing I could do is
stay by the phone and keep to my normal routine.
That way Shane knows how to contact me when
he's ready."

She knew she was letting herself in for more
heartbreak, but she had to ask. "Do you want
some company?"

"Yes, but I need you to stay there in case
Shane tries to contact you instead of me. He had a
better relationship with you than he had with
me."

"Are you sure, Levi? I wouldn't mind driving
to your place." He wanted her there! Things
couldn't be as hopeless as she thought.

"I'm sure. Get some sleep, but . . . well,
keep your ears open, okay?"

"Will I see you in the morning?"

"Yeah. Remember I'm supposed to keep a
normal schedule, and where else would I be besides your place?"

"I know this sounds inept, Levi, but try to get
some sleep. Shane's a smart boy, he won't be doing anything stupid."

"Yeah, well he must be getting that from his
father's side of the family. I managed to screw up
royally. You were right, Georgia. Some people
don't deserve children." He didn't wait for her
response, he just hung up.

She slowly replaced the receiver, hugged her knees tighter, and rocked.

Two exhausting and nerve-stretching days later, Georgia opened her door to find Shane standing there. Dusk had already fallen, and Levi had headed home for another night of alternately waiting by the phone and riding around the area. She blinked several times before believing her own eyes. "Shane!" She launched herself at the boy and hugged him so tightly she was afraid she might have cracked one or two of his ribs. "Where have you been?"

Shane shrugged and nervously passed his backpack from hand to hand. "Can I stay here?" He swallowed hard, straightened his shoulders, and admitted, "I don't have anywhere else to go."

"Of course you can." She pulled him into the living room before he had a chance to disappear again. He looked terrible. He had dark circles under his eyes, and he appeared to have lost weight. "Are you hungry?"

Her mind raced frantically. The first thing she had to do was make sure he was all right. Then she'd call Levi. "I have some spaghetti and meatballs left over from dinner." She had kept herself busy by cooking, but her appetite couldn't keep up with her busy hands. "There's even some garlic bread." She pulled Shane into the kitchen, pushed him onto one of the counter stools, and started to unload the refrigerator.

Shane's smile didn't reach his eyes. "I guess I'm staying for dinner."

"Count on it." She shoved bowls into the microwave and pushed the buttons like a pro. She tossed him two cookies from the batch she'd baked the night before and poured him a tall glass of milk. "You're always welcome here, Shane. You should know that."

"That's why I'm here." He downed the milk without coming up for air. "I take it my uncle's pretty mad at me about right now."

"No, your uncle isn't mad at you. Out of his mind with worry, yes, mad, no." She refilled the glass and this time left the carton on the counter. "Do you want to stay here with me, Shane, or do you want to go back to your uncle's?"

"Can I stay here with you? My relatives don't seem to want me." He stared down at the countertop. "I know we aren't related or anything, but I could work for my board."

Her heart caught so, she would have sworn the damn thing stopped beating for an instant. "Levi wants you very much, Shane, perhaps too much. Maybe that's what his problem is. I don't know."

Shane started to stand up. "You don't want me here either. That's okay, George, I under—"

"Sit down, Shane." She was surprised by his prompt response. He sat. "Of course, you can stay

here, if that's what you want. But there's got to be
some rules first."

"Like?"

"First, we'll call your uncle and tell him you're
here and safe."

"What if he says I have to come home?"

She picked up on his use of the word "home"
but didn't comment on it. "I'll talk to him about
it. I'm sure he'll let you stay once he knows you're
safe. Next, you are to go back to school tomorrow
morning, and there will be no more talk about
working for your board." She grabbed a plate and
piled a small mountain of reheated noodles, sauce,
and meatballs on it.

"That's it?" Shane reached for the plate and
fork and immediately dug in.

"You're going to have to make up the work
you missed in school."

He shrugged as if that was no problem and
continued to shovel food into his mouth as if he
hadn't eaten in days. She wondered if he had. He
looked as if he had been sleeping in the woods.
"You also need a shower, your clothes washed,
and please call Cynthia. The poor girl has been
driving Levi nuts with her phone calls. You'll be
happy to know she bothers your uncle about six
times a day checking on your whereabouts."

For the first time since entering her house,
Shane smiled as if he meant it. "She does?"

"Like clockwork." She placed two slices of

garlic bread near his plate. "Any reason why you didn't contact her or any of your other friends?"

"I didn't want to get them involved. Levi already hates them all, why give him more reasons?"

"That's not true, but I don't want to argue about it with you now. Let's call Levi and tell him where you are."

"Can you do it?"

"Don't you want to talk to him?"

"Maybe tomorrow I'll talk to him, but not right now." Shane stared down at his plate. "I don't know what to say to him."

"I think he's the one who has some talking to do, Shane. Not you." She patted his hand. "I'll call him now. You finish your dinner."

ELEVEN

Georgia glanced at the kitchen table for the fourth time and purposely removed the flowery centerpiece. It was too formal. She was aiming for a more homey and relaxing setting. She was perfectly comfortable with the flowers, but she didn't think her two dinner companions would share the sentiment. Levi and Shane would be more interested in what they were eating than which set of dishes she was using. She was more than willing to accommodate her guests. Today, Shane was finally willing to talk to Levi and hear what his uncle had to say.

The dinner had been her idea. Something simple and casual. A comfortable meal during which conversation would be encouraged. That morning, before he caught the bus to school, Shane had told her it was time for him and Levi to talk, but he wanted her there. She had suggested inviting Levi to dinner and Shane had agreed.

The past three days had been both a blessing and a curse for Georgia. Having Shane in her home was a joy. She'd never known how much she liked having someone to talk to at night or even just watch a television show with. Her brother's workday had always started early and ended late, and for the past several years she had been wrapped up in building her business.

The downside of Shane's "visit" was his impending departure. She was going to miss him terribly, but it would be for the best. Levi needed his nephew home. Anyone looking at the man could see his distress. When she had called him three nights ago, he had sounded relieved for Shane's safety, and resigned to the fact that the boy wanted to stay with her, for the time being. She had wished Shane would go back home for Levi's sake, but she was happy for the time to get to know the boy better. Shane was a polite, intelligent, and caring individual. Any parent would be proud to call him son.

The days had passed swiftly, with Shane attending school and staying after, both to catch up on some work and to avoid his uncle. Levi worked like a man possessed, only taking breaks to watch his nephew leave her house and board the bus and then arrive back home. They didn't work together.

Every morning after Shane left she entered

the barn and gave Levi a quick rundown on anything the boy might have done since the last time
she gave him a report. Levi sucked up every
ounce of information as if he were a sponge, but
he didn't force a meeting with Shane. He was
willing to wait until the boy was ready to talk to
him.

When she had invited Levi to dinner that
morning, telling him Shane was ready to talk, he
had hauled her into his arms and hugged her
tightly. He had simply held her and thanked her
over and over again. She had been moved to tears
and if she wasn't mistaken, so was he. Levi had
left the job site earlier than usual because he
wanted to go home and clean up before the meal.
He was due back any minute. Shane was up in the
spare bedroom talking to Cynthia on the phone,
and she was pacing the shine off her brand new
linoleum floor.

The sound of Levi pulling into her gravel
driveway snapped her out of the pacing. It was
show time. Levi was about to do anything to win
back his nephew. Shane wanted to be back in
Levi's life, he just wasn't sure how to go about it.
And she needed the two men in her life to work
out their differences. How could she ever become
part of their lives if they weren't together?

Forty minutes later Levi placed his fork on his
empty plate and declared, "That was delicious,

Georgia." He couldn't postpone the inevitable any longer; dinner had to end and with it the polite topics of conversation. For the past thirty-five minutes they had discussed the weather, the work on the barn, Shane's school, and tonight's football game, when the Cocalico Eagles would take on Donegal. Shane obviously wanted to go see Cynthia cheer their school to victory. If Levi wanted his nephew to catch the opening kickoff, he'd better start talking.

"Yeah, George," Shane said, "that was almost as good as the meatloaf you made last night."

"Thank you, both." Georgia started to gather up the dishes.

"Leave them for a moment, Georgia," Levi said. "I'll help clean up later." He looked at his nephew for a really long time before muttering, "I screwed up and I'm sorry."

Shane shrugged and looked embarrassed by his uncle's confession. "I shouldn't have taken off like that."

"If there's ever a next time, come directly to Georgia's. That way I'll know you're safe and in good hands." He gave Georgia a small smile and hoped he wasn't making a complete fool out of himself by thinking Shane would be coming home with him that night. "Thanks for picking up the pieces."

"It was my pleasure." Georgia smiled at Shane.

Levi nervously toyed with the handle of his

fork. He had to wonder if this was how Catholics felt when they went to confession. If so, he could understand why there was that screen between them and the priest. It was so much easier to talk when you didn't have to actually look at a person. "I guess I owe you an explanation for my recent behavior. I won't use the word excuse, because what I did and what I said to you and Georgia was inexcusable."

Georgia and Shane exchanged glances, but neither one spoke.

"I don't know if you remember, Shane, because you were just a little boy when it happened, but I was married once. Her name was Christine, and she was my high school sweetheart." He could feel Georgia's gaze but he focused on Shane. This apology was being directed at his nephew. Georgia's would come later. "Christine was, let's say the clingy type. She didn't want me going anywhere or doing anything without her. I didn't argue with her because that's what I thought boyfriends and girlfriends did. They became one unit, one person, one mind. She talked me out of going to college because she wouldn't be there. I joined a construction crew because the money was good and Christine liked to go places."

"No offense, Unc, but she sounds like a real b-i-t-c-h to me."

"Well, I was the one who listened to her. A couple years after we graduated I started to realize that we were heading in two different directions. I regretted not going to college, and Christine was wearing what little love was left between us into the ground. I was about to end our relationship when she informed me she was pregnant."

He heard Georgia gasp, but didn't dare look at her. "We were married the following month. Two months later I found out that Christine had lied. She hadn't been pregnant." He frowned down at his plate and wondered how he could make Shane understand how sacred marriage was to him. "I was raised in a very religious and proper family. Shane, you know your grandparents and the values they hold dear. I couldn't divorce Christine because she had lied. She was my wife, and as the vows went, we were together for better or for worse. I was willing to make a go at the marriage and at first, so was she. Over the next couple of years she left me a few times, but I always took her back. I know it sounds stupid or even weak, but it was how I was raised. Eleven years ago she left me for her lover and she filed for a divorce. I haven't seen her since."

He looked up at Shane. "I just recently realized I've been blaming her this whole time for stealing my youthful dreams of going to college and making something out of my life. She didn't steal my future, I let her have it. As it turned out, I made something out of my life. I built a business that I'm very proud of and that I love. Christine doesn't have the power to hurt me any longer, but

last Friday night she still did. I looked up and saw
you standing there with Cynthia and it was déjà
vu all over again." He gave his nephew a guilty
smile. "You see, Christine had blond hair and was
as cute as your Cynthia. She was also a cheerleader. Seeing you two together was like looking
into a time-warped mirror, and I panicked. I
didn't want you to go through what I went
through. I wanted you to have a future."

"So you thought Cynthia and Christine were
the same?" Shane asked.

"Something like that." What else could he
say?

"No offense, Unc, but you don't know nothing about babes." Shane glanced at Georgia and
quickly amended his statement. "I mean,
women."

Levi rolled his eyes. "Tell me about it."

Shane chuckled. "Cynthia's going to college.
She's going to be a doctor, and I wouldn't want to
try to talk her out of it."

"That's good. I wouldn't want you to."

"Besides, she has to do something while I'm
away at school."

Levi raised an eyebrow. He wasn't worried
about Shane's college tuition bills. There was a
nice size nest egg already set aside for his education from the sale of his parents' farm. "Any idea
on what you would be going for?"

Shane shrugged. "Veterinary Medicine."

Levi grinned. "Excellent choice. I know your parents would have approved."

Shane managed a small smile of his own. "Yeah, they would have." He pushed away his plate. "Now that you know Cynthia's not going to ruin my life, can I come home?"

"Yes." Levi breathed a huge sigh of relief. "You could have always come home, Shane. The door will always be open to you." He shrugged. "I'm not very good at this father business, so will you be patient with me?"

"Yeah, well, I guess that's going to work both ways, Unc." Shane looked at Georgia. "You won't mind my leaving?"

Georgia winked. "I'll manage."

"I ran away from Uncle Bert's house and they shipped me off to Grandma Lottie's to live."

"The only place I'll be shipping you to is home, Shane." Levi reached across the table, holding out his right hand. "Let's make a deal. No more running away or shipping anyone off when we have a problem. We'll talk about it like two adults."

Shane shook his hand. "Cool."

Levi glanced at the clock. It was almost seven. "Now that that's settled, if you want to go see Cynthia cheer on those football players, I'll drop you off at the stadium."

"What time do you want me home? The game's over around ten, and then a bunch of us want to go out to the diner to grab something to eat."

"Be back here at eleven-thirty. We can pack up your stuff then." He glanced at Georgia. "If that's okay with you?"

"That's fine." She stood and started once again to gather the plates.

Levi took them out of her hands. "Don't you dare clean up. You cooked. I'll do that as soon as I get back from dropping Shane off. You want to come with us?"

"No, you two go." She shooed them toward the door.

"Hey, Unc, know what I just realized?"

"I'm afraid to ask," he teased as he stepped out on the porch.

"Georgia's a blonde, just like Cynthia and Christine. Liking blondes must run in the family."

Levi could only muster a sick-sounding chuckle at Georgia's murderous glare as he headed for the truck with his nephew by his side. "Shane, there's an awful lot you don't know about women. And by Georgia's reaction to that comment, I'll be lucky if I live long enough to teach you any of it."

Georgia stood in the powder room and stared into the mirror. She liked her blond hair, but more important it was natural. She had been born with this color and as far as she was concerned, she'd die with it. Granted, it wasn't as light as it had been when she was little, but everyone knew how harmful it was to spend hours out in the sun. Maybe it was a coincidence that she and Levi's ex-wife both had blond hair. Millions of women had blond hair. There was nothing strange about that, was there?

A moment later she left the bathroom in disgust. She was being ridiculous. The kitchen needed her attention and she wasn't waiting for Levi to return. She started carrying over the dirty dishes and loading them into the dishwasher.

The evening had gone extremely well. Levi was getting Shane home and Shane was getting a nice healthy dose of unconditional love. If she were a doctor, she couldn't have ordered a better prescription.

Levi's revelations about his ex-wife and his past answered a lot of her questions. She now understood what had set him off last week, and in an offbeat way she could even understand. Picturing Levi as a teenager being led around by his hormones by a perky cheerleader wasn't too difficult. As he grew into a young man, it became a little harder.

The fake pregnancy had been a dirty and deceitful lie to get Levi down the aisle. She now understood his meticulous care in using protection every time they had made love. He wasn't looking forward to another shotgun wedding, especially if the shotgun was empty.

She placed the platter containing the remaining chicken on the counter, and laid her hand across her flat abdomen. Levi's child! The thought of carrying Levi's baby should have sent her into a hyperventilation attack. Instead she stood there staring down into the gravy boat with a silly smile on her face.

Levi's baby! It sounded so right. Felt so right.

"Hey, I thought I told you not to touch the dishes," Levi said as he walked into the room.

She dropped her hand and jumped a good four inches into the air. "Lord, Levi, don't scare me like that!"

"I didn't think I was being that quiet." He frowned at the completely cleared table and shook his head. Picking up the dishrag, he wiped the table, then placed the vase of yellow and white carnations back in the center of the table.

She dished the leftovers into containers and finished loading the dishwasher. "It's going to seem strange to have leftovers. Shane has a habit of raiding the refrigerator around ten-thirty every night."

"I know." He tossed the rag back into the sink. "Thanks again, Georgia, for being there when Shane needed you." He reached out and caressed her cheek. "When I needed you."

She leaned into the warmth of his hand. "As I said before, it was my pleasure."

Levi dropped his hand and tugged her over to the stools. He sat on one and nodded to the other. "I didn't tell Shane the whole story about Christine."

She sat. "You didn't?" She'd thought there was an awful lot left unsaid, but she hadn't expected Levi to air all his dirty laundry.

"The part about how we met and got married was true. Even the part about her leaving me for her lover and filing for a divorce was true. I just didn't tell him or you about Jenny."

"Jenny?"

"My daughter."

Instantly, her stomach clenched with an incredible ache of emptiness. Some other woman had carried Levi's baby. "You have a daughter?"

"No." He ran his fingers through his hair. "I mean yes. In my heart, Jenny is my daughter, will always be my daughter."

"No she isn't your daughter, but yes she is. Now, I'm really confused."

"Christine was playing her usual on-again, off-again marriage number when she came crying back to me. She swore she loved me and was ready to settle down and give me the family I'd been wanting. I took her back, but I told her it was the last time. We couldn't keep on going the way we were. I'm not sure if I would have kept to that or not."

He stared out the door and into the approaching evening. "Six weeks later she told me she was

pregnant and even proved it this time by taking
one of those home pregnancy tests. I was ecstatic
and she was miserable. First there was morning
sickness, then her clothes didn't fit, then she
gained weight by just breathing. Jennifer was
born over a month early and only weighed five
pounds two ounces. She was the most beautiful
little girl.

"Christine lost interest in Jenny immediately,
but I didn't mind too much. It left more time for
me to be with her. I worked all day at the construction site and took care of my sweet little
Jenny all night. Christine managed to hold it together at home for the hours that I worked. By
the time Jenny was four months old, Christine
was back to her old tricks."

Georgia felt a building rage that she'd never
experienced before. How could a woman do that
to her baby? What kind of woman had Levi
loved? "Did you still love Christine then?"

"No." He shook his head. "I was thankful and
tolerant of her because she had brought my
daughter into the world, nothing more." He
shrugged, but didn't offer any other excuses.
"When Jenny was eleven months old, Christine
informed me she was leaving me for the final
time. I told her to go, but she wasn't taking Jenny
with her. Then my darling wife informed me that
Jenny wasn't my child. That her current lover had
fathered her nearly two years earlier."

"And you believed her?"

"No, but the initial blood work told the truth. Jenny couldn't possibly be my daughter. We didn't need to wait for further DNA results. Christine left with Jenny ten years ago and I haven't seen them since."

She reached for his hand and squeezed. "I don't know what to say, Levi. I'm so sorry." My God, she thought. She had told this man that some people didn't deserve to be parents! She had been right, but that comment shouldn't have been directed at him, but at his ex-wife.

"So am I." He squeezed her hand in return but didn't let go of it. "It took me a long time to get over it. For a while I hid from the world, then I concentrated on starting my business. I kept my heart safe because I refused to risk it again. Then Shane entered my life and I found myself once again in the 'father' role. I know he's technically not my son, but he has my sister's blood running through his veins, so it's close. Closer than Jenny had been, and I loved her unconditionally."

She found herself blinking back tears. "I'm glad you and Shane have worked things out. You both need each other."

"It seems we need one more thing in our lives, Georgia. We both need you."

She could only stare at Levi. What was he saying?

"My heart has been doing some amazing things lately. Not only has it made room for Shane, but a certain antique store owner has managed to worm her way in also." He reached out and wiped a tear off her cheek. "I love you, Georgia. Maybe it's asking too much, but would you consider becoming part of Shane's and my life permanently?"

"As in marriage?"

"As in becoming a family." He hauled her off the stool and into his arms. "Marry me, Georgia?"

She threw her arms around his neck and shouted, "Yes!"

Forty minutes later Georgia was naked, satisfied, and deliciously happy in Levi's arms. There was a trail of clothes leading from the kitchen and up the stairs to her bedroom door. There the trail ended. Levi had been inside her before they made it to the bed.

She snuggled against his warmth. "I hope that football game goes into overtime."

Levi chuckled and glanced at the clock. "We have plenty of time." His hand slowly and suggestively caressed her hip.

She matched his chuckle with one of her own. "What do you have in mind?"

"Lord, woman, give me a minute to recover."

She pressed a kiss to the center of his chest. "I hate to be the one bringing this up, and it's like closing the barn door after the horse has gotten out, but we seem to have forgotten to use something this time." She wasn't sure if Levi had been caught up in the moment or if he had consciously not used a condom. The possibility that they might create a baby left her feeling strangely satisfied. Then again, the feeling could be sparked by his recent proposal or the earth-shattering climax she had just experienced.

"They're in the pocket of my pants, and if my memory serves me correctly you stripped me of my pants on the third step."

"So I did." He didn't sound too upset with the ramifications, and if anyone would know them, it would be he. She leaned up on her elbow and stared down into his handsome face. A face she would be seeing in her bed for the rest of her life. "You also never gave me the chance to tell you how much I love you."

He reached up and pulled her head down to his. "That's because your mouth was too busy purring like a kitten." He brushed her lips with his own.

"There's still one more thing I'm dying to know."

Strong, capable hands lifted her up so her breasts swung freely, mere inches from his mouth. "Ask away while you still have the time." He raised his head and captured a nipple between his lips.

She arched her back and straddled his waist with her thighs. "Do you really have a thing for blondes, or is it just a coincidence?"

"I have this things for blondes"—he chuckled and tugged on her other nipple—"named Georgia who purr like a kitten."

She wiggled her hips against his growing arousal and purred.

EPILOGUE

Georgia smiled at the reflection staring back at her from the floor-to-ceiling mirror. She looked beautiful. Hell, she looked radiant. The white satin and lace wedding gown fit her body with such perfection, it was exquisitely breathtaking. For the price the White Lace and Promises Bridal Boutique was charging her brother, who insisted on paying for her wedding, Cinderella's pumpkin coach should have come with it.

Morgan's reflection joined hers in the mirror. "You look beautiful, sis. Mom and Dad would have been so proud of you."

"For getting married?" She loved her brother dearly, but really. Women didn't consider nabbing a husband their crowning achievement.

"No, for the success you made of the stores, for turning out so unspoiled and beautiful." He leaned over and kissed her on the cheek. "Levi

Horst is one very lucky man." Morgan glanced toward the curtains, as if he were waiting for someone.

"Relax, Morgan, Levi is not going to storm in here and call off the wedding." She still couldn't believe her brother had insisted on accompanying her to the boutique for her final fitting.

"Why in the hell did you pick this place to buy your gown? Aren't the memories depressing?"

Poor Morgan, he still didn't understand. "No, the memories are wonderful." She laughed as her brother shook his head. "If Adam hadn't called off the wedding, I never would have purchased the house or the barn, and I never would have met Levi. I owe Adam a debt of gratitude."

"I owe him another black eye." Morgan stepped over the six-foot train of satin pooled on the ground behind her.

"Be thankful he didn't sue you for assault." She turned back to the mirror and smiled. This dress was so different from the one she'd had on months ago. This one felt right.

"Well, if Levi comes barging in here, I'll probably rip off his head."

"He won't be coming, Morgan." She placed her hand against her still flat abdomen and smiled. Last night, with the wedding a mere week away, she had confided to Levi the secret she had been hoarding for the past month from fear he would think she was pressuring him into this marriage. They were going to have a baby. By Levi's joyous reaction to that news, she knew that nothing and no one would be keeping him from the church on Saturday.

"What makes you so confident this time?"

She studied her brother for a moment. He seemed to be asking the question for a personal reason, as if he was curious to know why she was willing to risk it all. "Love, Morgan." She reached up and kissed his cheek. "You should try it sometime."

THE EDITORS' CORNER

People often ask how we can keep track of all the LOVESWEPTs, the authors and their stories, and good grief, all the characters! It's actually pretty easy. We're fortunate to have some of the most talented authors writing for us, telling beautiful stories about memorable and endearing characters. To lose track of them would be like losing track of what's going on in the lives of our closest friends! The August LOVESWEPT lineup is no exception to the rule. We hope you enjoy these stories as much as we did!

First up is Loveswept favorite Laura Taylor, who leaves us all breathless with **ANTICIPATION**, LOVESWEPT #846. Viva Conrad fled Kentucky without warning, leaving behind a life she adored and silencing her dreams in a gamble to keep the people she loved safe. Spencer Hammond will stop at nothing to discover the truth of her desertion and her involvement in his stepbrother's death. Brought together by the wishes of a dead man and a racehorse guaranteed to win it all, Viva and Spencer must learn to tolerate each other for the good of their investment. As their individual agendas collide, the two must also deal with the unexpected attraction that flares to life between them, amid secrets that threaten to destroy what they long to build together. Suspense rivals sensuality in Laura Taylor's riveting saga of dangerous secrets and shadowy seductions.

Next on the docket, Peggy Webb returns with an exciting romp through the southern part of heaven with a man who can only be referred to as Tarzan on a Harley. After having headed for the hills to forget a thoughtless scoundrel, B. J. Corban is now stuck with the job of **BRINGING UP BAXTER**, LOVESWEPT #847. Baxter, you see, is this cute little puppy who's trying to steal everyone's heart (and the limelight as well). However, when B. J. gets a look at the muscular legs encased in the tight leather pants of Crash Beauregard, she scents danger and irresistible possibilities. Prim lawyer that she is, B. J. tries to resist the devilish charms of the sexy rebel. Peggy teases and tempts with delicious wit and delectable humor as she reveals just what happens when a big-city lawyer and a judge from the sticks tangle over a case of true love.

Detective Aaron Stone desperately needs a break in the murder investigation of notorious drug dealer Owen Blake in **BLACK VELVET**, LOVESWEPT #848 by Kristen Robinette. So when a phone call comes through for the deceased dealer, Aaron jumps on this new lead. On a lark, Katherine Jackson tries to contact the man of her dreams, just to see if he really exists. When they meet, the attraction sizzles and Aaron must now decide whether this woman with the face of an angel bears the heart of a killer. Katherine's dreams begin to reveal more secrets, this time involving Aaron. These secrets evoke more emotions than Aaron can bear and it's up to Katherine to give him new hope where none had seemed possible. Kristen Robinette's story is woven of equal parts mesmerizing mystery and heartbreaking emotion and is guaranteed to touch your heart, as a man's heart is slowly healed by the love of his life.

Please welcome newcomer Kathy DiSanto, who gives us a story about a man struggling to decide if women want him **FOR LOVE OR MONEY**, LOVESWEPT #849. Acting on a dare has never worked out well for teacher Jennifer Casey. But when she's *triple-dog* dared to write a letter to millionaire Brent Maddox, her pride leaves her no choice. When he shows up at her doorstep with a dare of his own, Jen must spend a week with Brent in his "natural habitat" to see how the other half lives. Hobnobbing with the rich and famous has taught Jen that their lives are vastly different from hers, but can Brent teach her otherwise? As their tempers collide and their hearts unite, Jen and Brent must build a bridge between their two worlds. Kathy's romantic tale of two unlikely lovers is fast-paced and funny—and one you'll never forget!

By now you guys must have seen the new LOVESWEPT look. We hope you are as pleased with it as we are. Please let us know what you think by writing to us in care of Joy Abella, or even visiting our BDD Online web site (http://www.bdd.com/romance)!

Happy reading!

With warmest regards,

Shauna Summers   Joy Abella

Shauna Summers   Joy Abella
Editor   Administrative Editor

P.S. Look for these Bantam women's fiction titles coming in August. From Deborah Smith, one of the freshest voices in romantic fiction, comes **A PLACE TO CALL HOME**, an extraordinary love story begun in childhood friendship and rekindled after twenty years of separation. Bestselling author Jane Feather is back with **THE SILVER ROSE**, the second book in her "Charm Bracelet Trilogy," a tale of two noble families, the legacy of an adulterous passion, and the feud that threatens to spill more blood . . . or bind two hearts against all odds.

From the bestselling author of *Breath of Magic* and *Shadows and Lace* comes a beguiling new time-travel love story in the hilarious, magical voice that has made

Teresa Medeiros

one of the nation's most beloved romance writers.

TOUCH OF ENCHANTMENT

Heiress Tabitha Lennox considered her paranormal talents a curse, so she dedicated her life to the cold, rational world of science. Until the day she examined the mysterious amulet her mother left her and found herself catapulted seven centuries into the past—directly into the path of a chain-mailed warrior. . . . Sir Colin of Ravenshaw had returned from the Crusades to find his enemy poised to overrun the land where his family had ruled for generations. The last thing he expected was to narrowly avoid trampling a damsel with odd garb and even odder manners. But it is her strange talent that will create trouble beyond Colin's wildest imaginings. For everyone knows that a witch must be burned—and Colin's heart is already aflame. . . .

He thought the creature was female, but he couldn't be sure. Any hint of its sex was buried beneath a shapeless tunic and a pair of loose leggings. It blinked up at him, its gray eyes startlingly large in its pallid face.

"Who the hell are you?" he growled. "Did that murdering bastard send you to ambush me?"

It lifted its cupped hands a few inches off the ground. "Do I look like someone sent to ambush you?"

The thing had a point. It wore no armor and carried no weapon that he could see, unless you counted those beseeching gray eyes. Definitely female, he decided with a grunt of mingled relief and pain. He might have been too long without a woman, but he'd yet to be swayed by any of the pretty young lads a few of his more jaded comrades favored.

He steadied his grip on the sword, hoping the woman hadn't seen it waver. His chest heaved with exhaustion and he was forced to shake the sweat from his eyes before stealing a desperate glance over his shoulder.

The forest betrayed no sign of pursuit, freeing him to return his attention to his trembling captive. "Have you no answer for my question? Who the hell are you?"

To his surprise, the surly demand ignited a spark of spirit in the wench's eyes. "Wait just a minute! Maybe the question should be, Who the hell are *you*?" Her eyes narrowed in a suspicious glare. "Don't I know you?" She began to mutter beneath her breath as she studied his face, making him wonder if he hadn't snared a lunatic. "Trim the hair. Give him a shave and a bath. Spritz him with Brut and slip him into an off-the-rack suit. Aha!" she crowed. "You're George, aren't you? George . . . George . . . ?" She snapped her fingers. "George Ruggles from Accounting!" She slanted him a glance that was almost coy. "Fess up now, Georgie boy. Did Daddy offer you a raise to play knight in shining armor to my damsel in distress?"

His jaw went slack with shock as she swatted his sword aside and scrambled to her feet, brushing the grass from her shapely rump with both hands. "You can confide in me, you know. I promise it won't affect your Yearly Performance Evaluation."

She was taller than he had expected, taller than any woman of his acquaintance. But far more disconcerting than her height was her brash attitude. Since he'd been old enough to wield a sword, he'd never met anyone, man or woman, who wasn't afraid of him.

The sun was beating down on his head like an anvil. He clenched his teeth against a fresh wave of pain. "You may call me George if it pleases you, my lady, but 'tis *not* my name."

She paced around him, making the horse prance and shy away from her. "Should I call you Prince then? Or will Mr. Charming do? And what would you like to call me? Guenevere perhaps?" She touched a hand to her rumpled hair and batted her sandy eyelashes at him. "Or would you prefer Rapunzel?"

His ears burned beneath her incomprehensible taunts. He could think of several names he'd like to call her, none of them flattering. A small black cat appeared out of nowhere to scamper at her heels, forcing him to rein his stallion in tighter or risk trampling them both. Each nervous shuffle of the horse's hooves jarred his aching bones.

She eyed his cracked leather gauntlets and tarnished chain mail with blatant derision. "So where's your shining armor, Lancelot? Is it back at the condo being polished or did you send it out to the dry cleaners?"

She paced behind him again. All the better to slide a blade between his ribs, he thought dourly. Resisting the urge to clutch his shoulder, he wheeled the horse around to face her. The simple motion made his ears ring and his head spin.

"Cease your infernal pacing, woman!" he bellowed.

"Or I'll—" He hesitated, at a loss to come up with a threat vile enough to stifle this chattering harpy.

She flinched, but the cowed look in her eyes was quickly replaced by defiance. "Or you'll what?" she demanded, resting her hands on her hips. "Carry me off to your castle and ravish me? Chop my saucy little head off?" She shook her head in disgust. "I can't believe Mama thought I'd fall for this chauvinistic crap. Why didn't she just hire a mugger to knock me over the head and steal my purse?"

She marched away from him. Ignoring the warning throb of his muscles, he drove the horse into her path. Before she could change course again, he hefted his sword and nudged aside the fabric of her tunic, bringing the blade's tip to bear against the swell of her left breast. Her eyes widened and she took several hasty steps backward. He urged the stallion forward, pinioning her against the trunk of a slender oak. As her gaze met his, he would have almost sworn he could feel her heart thundering beneath the blade's dangerous caress.

A mixture of fear and doubt flickered through her eyes. "This isn't funny anymore, Mr. Ruggles," she said softly. "I hope you've kept your résumé current, because after I tell my father about this little incident, you'll probably be needing it."

She reached for his blade with a trembling hand, stirring reluctant admiration in him. But when she jerked her hand back, her fingertips were smeared with blood.

At first he feared he had pricked her in his clumsiness. An old shame quickened in his gut, no less keen for its familiarity. He'd striven not to harm any woman since he'd sworn off breaking hearts.

She did not yelp in distress or melt into a swoon. She simply stared at her hand as if seeing it for the first time. "Doesn't feel like ketchup," she muttered, her words even more inexplicable than her actions. She sniffed at her fingers. "Or smell like cherry cough syrup."

She glanced down at her chest. A thin thread of blood trickled between her breasts, affirming his fears. But as her bewildered gaze met his and the ringing in his ears deepened to an inescapable roaring, he realized what she had already discovered. 'Twas not her blood staining her breast, but his own. His blood seeping from his body in welling drops that were rapidly becoming a steady trickle down the blade of his sword. Horror buffeted him as he realized it was he, and not she, who was in danger of swooning. The sword slipped from his numb fingers, tumbling harmlessly to the grass.

He slumped over the horse's neck, clutching at the coarse mane. He could feel his powerful legs weakening, betrayed by the weight of the chain mail that was supposed to protect him. Sweat trickled into his eyes, its relentless sting blinding him.

"Go," he gritted out. "Leave me be."

At first he thought she would obey. He heard her skitter sideways, then hesitate, poised on the brink of flight.

His flesh felt as if it were tearing from his bones as he summoned one last burst of strength to roar, "I bid you to leave my sight, woman. Now!"

The effort shredded the tatters of his will. He could almost feel his pride crumbling along with his resolve, forcing him to choke out the one word he detested above all others. "Please . . ."

Swaying in the saddle, he pried open his eyes to cast her a beseeching glance. Sir Colin of Ravenshaw had never fallen before anyone, especially not a woman.

And in the end he didn't fall before this one either.

He fell on her.

Sometimes the only thing standing in the way of true love is true friendship. . . .

REMEMBER THE TIME

by Annette Reynolds

An emotional, powerful story that celebrates all the joys, fears, and passions of true love.

They were the best of friends since high school, an inseparable threesome: Kate Moran, Paul Armstrong, and Mike Fitzgerald. But it was Paul who won Kate's heart and married her, leaving Mike to love Kate from afar. Then, in a tragic accident, Paul died, and for Kate, it was as if she had lost her life, too. Now, after nearly three years of watching Kate mourn, of seeing the girl who loved life become a woman who suffers through it, Mike knows he can't hold back any longer. The time has come to tell her how he feels. And all he can hope is that Kate recognizes what he's known all along: that they've always been perfect for each other. But there are secrets that can shake even the strongest bonds of love and friendship . . . and betrayals that can tear two lovers apart.

The breeze blowing in from the open window had turned chilly and it woke her. The stiffness in her back brought an involuntary groan, a sound she didn't remember making when she was younger. Like gray hairs and laugh lines that suddenly appeared in her mid-thirties, so these new noises came, too.

The telephone that sat on the end table jangled. It was an old rotary phone from the forties, and she always swore she could see it wiggle and dance as the bell rang. Her cartoon phone. When she picked up, there was no one on the other end. This was a regular occurrence. The C & P Telephone Company—the initials stood for Chesapeake and Potomac but most residents called it Cheapskate and Poky—also seemed to date back to the forties. Kate hung up and waited for it to ring again. And it did.

"Kate? It's Mike. Didn't you see my note?"

"What note?" She could tell by the silence that Mike had closed his eyes in annoyance, and she said, "I heard that."

"I left a note by your front door."

"Where?" she continued to bait him.

"On a pushpin right next to the door. It was on a pink flyer for the SPCA Thrift Shop."

"I guess I didn't realize it was something important. What did it say?"

He picked up on her mood. His voice, a well-moderated blend of East Coast inflection with just a touch of Virginia gentleman, took on a slight Irish lilt. Kate called it his leprechaun voice. "They're havin' their annual half-off sale this weekend."

"What are you talking about?"

She didn't seem to be amused. He must have misjudged her. "Never mind. The gist of the note is that Homer is over here visiting me."

She sighed. "I thought it was a little too quiet."

"He got through that hole in the fence again. I can fix it for you, if you want." There was no reply. "Or not. Do you want me to bring him over?"

"If you must."

"I'm afraid I must. Are you decent?"

She smiled at that. It was a very old joke between them. "Never. Come on over."

Kate was still sitting on the couch when the front door opened four minutes later. She heard Homer's toe-nails scrabble across the hardwood floor of the entry hall as he raced to the kitchen, and his food bowl. He never understood why it wasn't perpetually full.

Mike's voice reached her. "Kate? Where are you?"

"In here."

"Where?"

"Just follow the sound of my voice."

"My, we're in a good mood," Mike said, entering the den. He took in her rumpled shirt and puffy eyes. Her dark auburn hair, which usually hung in gleaming waves to her shoulders, had been pulled back in a barrette that now stuck out at an angle. Wisps of hair had escaped and formed odd cowlicks. "And you got all dolled up just for me. You really shouldn't have."

"Nice to see you, too." As she spoke the words, her hands went to the barrette and removed it. She ran her fingers through her hair. "I was taking a nap."

Mike leaned against the built-in bookcase and folded his arms across his chest. "Late dinner for two last night?"

Kate eyed him for a split second, then retorted, "Yeah, me and David Letterman."

"Y'know, if you actually went to sleep before two A.M. you wouldn't wake up feeling like crap every day."

"Don't start, Mike. And not that it's any of your business, but I do go to sleep before two A.M."

"Falling asleep on the couch with the TV on isn't what I'd call getting a good night's sleep."

Almost too weary to argue, Kate fixed him with a look that would crumble stone. "I don't need another mother, thanks. And how the hell do you know where I sleep?"

"I got in late last night. Saw the light."

"What is it with you Fitzgeralds? If you're going to lecture me like I'm a child, then you can go home now."

Not wanting to be banished, he unfolded his arms and held them up in surrender. "Hey, I'm sorry. Can we start over?"

Kate looked down at the carpet. "Yeah, sorry. It's been a bad day." Her head came up and she tried to smile. "I could use a cup of coffee. Want one?"

Mike angled his body into one of the kitchen chairs and, with his foot, pulled another chair toward him and propped his long legs on it. Homer, always glad for any company, sat at his side and let Mike scratch his head.

Kate measured coffee into the filter and then took the carafe to the sink. Forgetting the cold water tap was practically welded shut, she grunted when it wouldn't turn. Swearing under her breath, she set the pot down to free both hands. It still wouldn't budge and Mike, hiding a grin, asked, "Can I get that for you?"

"Thanks, but I can do it," she answered, removing the pliers from the drawer.

He shook his head, but didn't say anything.

Once the coffee was perking, Kate realized she still hadn't started the dishwasher. Pulling two mugs out of the top rack, she began washing them.

"Are you sure this isn't too much trouble? We could always go to The Beverley."

Kate turned and gave him a warning look as she dried the mugs with a paper towel. All the dishcloths were in the dryer.

Setting a mug on the table next to him, she asked, "You take milk, right?"

He nodded and watched her open the refrigerator.

She stood in front of it for what seemed a very long time, and Mike suddenly understood why. "Hey, I can drink it black if you're out."

"No!" Her voice wavered momentarily. "No, I must have something you can use."

Mike's legs slipped off the chair and he sat up. "It's okay. Really."

She had closed the door and moved to the cupboards, her hands pushing aside cans and jars. Mike stood as she began frantically pawing through drawers. When her fingers closed around a small packet, she felt triumphant, until she saw it was a Wash'n Dri. Slamming it down on the counter, the tears finally came. Mike's hand on her shoulder made her flinch.

"Stop it, Kate. Forget it."

"I know I'll find something," she said between sobs.

"Katie, darlin', I can't stand to see you like this."

Her voice took on a hard edge. "Then go home, 'cause this is what I am now."

It took all the strength he had not to pull her to him. "I don't think you need to be alone."

"I think I know what I need."

"Christ, but you are pigheaded." He took a deep breath. "Do you really want me to go?" he asked, not wanting to hear her answer.

She nodded. "Yeah—go."

He stared at the back of her head before turning away. He left the way he came. It took her a few moments to realize she'd forgotten to thank him. Picking up one of the two clean mugs, she flung it across the room. It hit the stove top, shattering. Homer slunk out of the room, leaving her alone. It was what she wanted, after all. Wasn't it?

◆———————◆

He had loved her—no, make that obsessed over her—for as long as he could remember. It was their junior year. She had walked into their English class that first week of October—her family had just moved to the area—and she captured the heart of every male in the room.

The teacher introduces her as Kathleen Moran and asks her to tell the class a little about herself. With a tremendous amount of poise, she walks to the teacher's desk, puts down her purse and books, and says,

"Hi. I just moved here from Oklahoma but I was born in Pennsylvania. My father just retired from the Army and we're in Staunton because he's going to be teaching at the military academy. This is the eighth school I've gone to, but so far it seems like the friendliest." She looks at the faces watching her and notices a familiar one. It is a girl named Chris who lives across the street from her. They have already spoken and so she focuses on her when she says, "I've lived in five states and one foreign country but I've never seen any place as pretty as Staunton. And, by the way, everyone calls me Kate."

Her smile encompasses the entire room. It is impossible not to smile back at her. The boys have seen all they need to know about Kate Moran. Their minds are filled with ideas on how to make this auburn-haired beauty feel welcome. The girls' minds, however, are filled with other, less-than-charitable, ideas. And yet they find themselves smiling at her, too. Chris, Kate's first acquaintance, has already spread the word about this newcomer but nothing has prepared them for what she looks like. Chris's assessment of the situation had been, "You won't like her when you see her, but once you talk to her, she's pretty cool."

The teacher waits for the whispers to subside, then says, "Maybe you can tell us about some of your interests."

Kate has already picked up her belongings from the

teacher's desk and is walking toward an empty desk, when she tosses off, "Oh, I like rock music, reading, antiques. But I love baseball." She carefully slides her miniskirted body into the seat. All male eyes move their field of vision down a foot. "Especially the San Francisco Giants." Kate takes a pencil out of her purse, opens her spiral notebook, and looks up at the teacher expectantly.

"Yes. Well. Thank you, Kate." He has to physically pull himself away from her dark blue eyes. "We're glad to have you here."

Paul Armstrong leans forward and taps Mike on the shoulder. Best friends since the third grade, Mike knows what Paul is going to say before the words are out of his mouth.

"I think I'm in love," Paul whispers. It is his standard remark, made in his usual offhand way. This time he means it.

"You and me both, bud. Think she can handle the Dynamic Duo?" comes Mike's conditioned response. He keeps his voice light, but his heart feels heavy. He really wants this one, but Kate Moran seems to be made for Paul. And they agreed a long time ago not to let a girl get in the way of their friendship.

What did they know at the age of sixteen? They were young and stupid. And in the end it didn't really matter anyway. Kate had come into the lives of Paul and Mike not knowing the rules, and when Paul Armstrong saw her that crisp October day, the rule book got tossed out the window.

Mike held a glass of J & B as he stared out the bay window in his bedroom. With all the leaves off the trees, he had a clear view of her house. The only light he could see came from the den. It seemed to be the only room she used anymore. His sister had told him that she hadn't slept in the bedroom she'd shared with Paul since his death. Kate kept her clothes there and used it as a rather large dressing room, but that was it.

There was a living room and dining room. Both were formal. Packed with antiques that Kate had collected throughout her travels with Paul, they reminded Mike of some of the historic homes he'd visited. Filled with beautiful furnishings, but never used, they seemed like stage settings waiting for the players to make their entrance and bring them to life. Paul and Kate used to give legendary parties. Now, no one entered those rooms.

She had two guest rooms on the second floor. They were at the back of the house, and he guessed she slept in one of them when she wasn't using the couch in the den. Like most Victorian houses, it had one very large bathroom on the second floor, and a very tiny W.C. on the main floor. And, finally, there was the little tower room. He'd been in it only once, when he and Paul had moved some old boxes of papers out of the den. It had been in the dead of winter and they could see their breath as they piled the five years' worth of tax paperwork in a corner. At the time it seemed that the room contained all the usual things people had in their attics . . . Christmas decorations, old clothing that no one wanted, a shelf covered with magazines, and broken things that needed mending that no one ever got around to.

Mike brought the highball glass to his lips and sipped the scotch. The ice had melted. It tasted like warm medicine, and he grimaced. Finishing it in one gulp, he turned from the window and went back downstairs to wait for Sheryl and his nephew, Matt. He hadn't seen the boy in nearly a year and he was looking forward to it. He had wanted to invite Kate over, too. That was, rather apparently, out of the question.

On sale in July:

A PLACE TO CALL HOME
by **Deborah Smith**

THE SILVER ROSE
by **Jane Feather**